DEAD or ALIVE

By Judithe Williamson

ISBN: 9798731171397

Chapter 1

David came awake with a start, wondering where he was. He wasn't sure, but it was dark in here, and there appeared to be a woman in a chair near his bed. "Hey" he shouted, "Is anyone here?" He tried to sit up but found he was extremely weak, he vaguely remembered being hit with something very hard, and as he fell he heard voices. Unsure as to his where abouts, he tried again to sit up.

Paula moved her chair around and excitedly called out. "Yes, I'm here. So you finally woke up, we have been so worried about you."

"Who are you," he asked? "In fact where am I?"

"I'm Paula, I brought you here because you were hurt bad and this is where you wanted me to bring you."

"Well, I don't recall anyone named Paula. Also, you still haven't told me

Where 'here' is. What do you mean I was hurt, how did I get hurt? Was I driving or did I fall?"

"David let me call Steve and maybe he can tell you more."

"Wait, who is this Steve? In fact, you just called me 'David', where did you hear that name? It is not my name, my name is------, I don't seem to remember, but David doesn't sound right."

"You are David   Miles, and you are a policeman, in fact, you are a detective. Just let me call Steve and the Doctor, it will only take a minute."   Paula turned and left by the door calling to Steve Wilson and the doctor. It was unusual for the doctor to be there, but Steve had asked him to come so they could discuss David's condition.

"But Doctor Roberts, suppose he doesn't wake up, after all, it has been nearly a month already. We still don't know for sure if he will wake up as a ghost or be alright."

"Excuse me for interrupting but David is awake and doesn't know who I am or where he is."

Dr. Roberts arose from his seat at the table and followed Steve into

the next room. They both used the door, the doctor seemed to act more alive when he was with Steve, he had coffee and sat rather than float around the room.

"David," shouted Steve. "I was afraid I would never see you alive again. "But here you are, how do you feel? Can you remember what happened? We have very little to go on up to now."

"Who the hell are you, and why does everyone keep calling me David?

I don't know where I am nor why I am here, but if you will just   bring me some clothes, I can leave."

Dr. Roberts went toward David and gently took his wrist, counting his heart rate.   "He seems to have a strong heart rate, but for some reason, he appears to be agitated. We need to calm him down or he will undo all that we have done for him so far."

"Hey what are you doing, it feels as if someone or something is holding my arm. "

"David, it's alright Old man, I'm here and nothing will happen. I promise, thank God Paula found you in time and brought you here. But you have been in a coma for so long we were getting really worried, That's why the Doctor was here just now. He is right beside you and just testing your vitals.”

"If the Doctor is here why can’t I see him. Listen whoever you are I don’t

know you, and there isn’t a doctor beside me either. I don’t know what kind of a scam you’re running but I don’t want any part of it.   As soon as I can find my clothes, you can color me gone. Is that Paula part of this scheme

I see she didn’t come back in with you, so tell her for me thanks but no thanks.”

"Alright I will see to it you have some clothes. It is fine that you can’t see the doctor, or don’t know me, after all, you have been in a coma for nearly a   month. But before I get your clothes you will have to answer a couple of questions for me. Where are you going when you leave here? If you don’t remember who I am or who Paula is, then who are you?”

"I knew there was a reason you had me locked in here.”

"Locked? Did you try the door? We have been friends since grade school, you are a detective with the 27th   precinct. I worked there with you for a couple of years, and now I am a private detective, and (we), that is you and I have been solving some cold cases. We also have solved a couple of cases that weren't so cold and broke up a gang that was getting help in their operations from some big wigs in local government agencies. We have been speculating that it was some of their boys or one of the gang members themselves that had you killed. At least no one other than us knows if you are alive or dead yet. I figure if we can keep it this way for a time, then we can figure out who did what."

Suddenly the door flew open and a young girl hurled herself across the room and straight into David's arms. Talking with the same amount of energy as she displayed running. "Oh Uncle David you're getting better and we won't have to worry so much. It's all right if you get dead like mommy, but it's so much better if you are alive. Are you hungry, Aunt Deanna cooks really good and we can make you something. I'm learning to cook too."

"I know you, You're Krista and you're 8 years old. But how I know you I really don't know. You just called me Uncle David, am I a real relative?"

"No, but, my dad isn't really my dad either and my mother is a ghost. So what can I say,   to me you are my Uncle David, but if you don't want to be then I guess I won't call you that again. But who are you then and what should I call you?"

"No I don't mean that, but something is wrong with me and I don't know who I am really. Just be patient with me for awhile please, maybe you are the answer to me so I can find who I really am."

"Well then are you hungry, you've been sick for a long time, and sometimes when I was in that other house; I would have to go for one or two days without food. I was hungry all the time, but if I asked for food they would say I was just lazy and didn't deserve to have food like the rest of the people had. But I learned to steal (whoops) I wasn't supposed to tell that I stole things, But I really did, it was only an old crust of bread and I had a whole apple once too. But Dad and Aunt Deanna told me to eat lots, so I can have anything I want. It's so nice here I'm warm and Christmas came and brought me more clothes and another coat and shoes with socks and I got a doll from Santa Claus. So you see it's okay to be hungry, they feed you really good."

"You wonderful child all the bad stuff is over, and good things are ahead of you now. How fortunate you are and you still smile and bring joy to all of us. Yes please call me uncle David, I hope you will always keep smiling and bring joy to all around you. Yes, now that you mention it I am hungry. What do you think I would like to eat? I will leave it up to you as I think you are very smart for your age."

"Once when you were very tired I ordered French toast for you, but I think you have been sick for a long time so you need more to eat than that. Krista scrunched up her face in such a way that even Steve laughed at 'her' "   I think you should have some eggs but not too greasy so we will cook them in water and give you some toast with a little jelly and a cup of coffee. Then later we will give you more food, not too fast so it won't make you sick again." Krista then ran out to tell Deanna what he would like to eat.

"I don't know what I did to deserve a (niece), like that; but I am sure glad I did. If I may would you please, hand me those pants, I see there and a shirt?"

"I feel this is not a good idea as you have not even stood up in some time now. But I will be here if you need me." Steve handed the clothes to David, and stepped back, far enough to allow for some privacy but not too far incase he was needed.

David managed to put his pants on but was a little groggy and unsteady on his feet. "I guess I am a little bit off my legs as yet, but so far so good." He got his shirt wrapped around him and began the chore of buttoning his shirt up, but found he couldn't manage the buttons. "Maybe I will just sit here a few minutes, it seems I need to go a little slower."

"Would you like some help," asked Paula?

Chapter 2

"Did you just hear someone talking," David asked? "I thought I heard a woman's voice, but I don't see anyone. You told me earlier that there were ghosts here and I don't really believe in them but now I am beginning to wonder. Yes, mam, I would like some help with the buttons they seem to be giving me some trouble."

"Oh, David it is because you have been sick for so long and of course you will be weak for a time yet. But as long as you need me I will be here for you."

"Maybe I'm dead already and if not, I guess I will never want to leave this place. Because I can see an angel and the most beautiful angel ever. Miss whatever your name is, where are you from. Does everyone get you when they die, because if they do I will be very jealous?"

"So at least you can see me and hear me now, that's progress. If those pants and things are a little large it is because I haven't gone to your apartment to bring back some that should fit you better."

"You know where my apartment is? If I made any rude or ungentlemanly passes at you please forgive me. I rarely see a lady like you and I wouldn't want to do anything unseemly. Is that where I got hurt?   Was someone else making a pass and I stepped in?   Believe me, I'm not usually a bad person."

"Here is your food Uncle David, Aunt Deanna wouldn't let me carry it in she was afraid I would spill it, But I carried your coffee alone."

"Tell me little one, how come you call Deanna aunt and Steve Dad? They're married aren't they?"

"Yes, but when Aunt Deanna rescued me from that other place, she told me about my real mother and said I could call her Aunt. But then when those bad guys came after you and dad, My mother came too and made my real father sign some papers so Steve could be my dad. Don'tcha remember Uncle David? You were there too and that man had a gun, but you and Steve,   my new Dad, made them drop their guns and the other police men came too and put those handcuffs on them and took them away."

"I wish I could honey, but maybe after I feel a little better it will all come back to me." David got up then to set his plate on a stand and pick up his coffee, but suddenly he put his hand to his head and collapsed, Steve with the doctors help and Paula managed to get him up off from the floor and Deanna folded his bed open neatly as they laid him back down.

"Don't Anyone make any remarks about my cooking doing this?"

"Well honey he was awake and talking before he ate," grinned Steve.

"Fine, Just wait until supper time You're getting mud pies and raw carrots, and that's just the first course."

"Oh that sounds wonderful, " quipped Steve. As he grabbed her and spun her around the room. "Have you finished making the plans for our spring wedding?"

Deanna was laughing at him by this time. "Yes, should we tell everyone that we are just renewing our old vows? After all, we have been married for over a month ."

"As long as no matter how long it takes, I still get to keep you. And I am still not sorry that we got married by a justice of Peace, so no one would think bad things of you and we didn't take a chance on losing Krista."

"I feel the same way, I'm just sorry I had to marry that jerk first. But then we probably would have never met if I hadn't."

Just then the door burst open and an extremely upset Amanda came in crying, with another ghost close to her heels.

"Amanda, calm down and tell us what the trouble is," soothed Deanne.

"I'm sorry, we just see so much up here," she hiccuped." If

I had only known what was happening to her and others I am sure there was something we could have done. Oh by the way this is Kerri she has been trying to reach us but there was some sort of force field that was preventing her from reaching us. Steve, there is the baby to consider, this time and I don't know what to do about it. Can you come right away please, even though you are concerned about David?"

"Go with her Steve", said Dr. Roberts. "Paula and I have this end of things covered. David should sleep for a while now. I think his body was fighting him. First, there was the trauma of not being able to help the girls when he was beaten so severely, then wanting to let go as it was easier and seemed to release some of the pressure from the pain. Eventually, he would cross over, but his body or something or even possibly someone was holding him here so he continues to fight. At least he has been awake now and gotten some solid food in his system. He may sleep off and on for a couple of days, it is hard to say but things are better because he is asleep instead of in a coma. I believe that letting Little Krista come in from time to time when he is awake may be good for him. I also think it is a combination of everything that has given him a form of amnesia and he will snap out of it on his own, So go with the girls and know that David is in good hands, I believe he will be fine he still needs rest is all.   "

"Thank you, Doctor.   Paula, I am leaving Krista here sort of check on her from time to time, please. She should be fine on her own, but you never know what weird slime balls are out there and is mad at me because they got caught. I want Deanna with me, as we don't know for sure what we may be getting in to and Amanda said it was something about a baby. I'll keep in touch and let you know what is happening. Oh yes, stupid me, someone will let you know, as I am sure our heavenly gathering will be there to oversee it all."

"Amanda knows of a good and trustworthy

Doctor that is still among the living and can be trusted. Just have her contact him if you need to, I wish he had been around all those years ago when I needed help. I understand he is a very good man and I would be proud to meet him someday."

Amanda and Steve left in his old truck, having no idea as to where they were going. Deanna rode next to Steve with Kerri and Amanda pointing out the way.   A couple of miles away from town they came to an old abandoned barn. Here they stopped with Amanda making sure that Steve parked out of sight at least somewhat. They all approached the barn quietly, and let themselves in a side entrance. The place had been turned into a prison of sorts. Tied to a bed by one arm and another tie was around her ankle was a young woman of about 18 to 20 something. She was dirty and wore what had at one time been a party dress. Now it was only rags, and a couple of blankets were thrown off to one side. She lay there very still and in the dim light, Deanna could see movement coming from the bed near the woman. Running quickly toward the woman she saw a baby, that appeared to have been born a short time before. "Oh Steve," whispered Deanna, "This child has just been born, and is crying so hard. Can we get it or what are we to do? It also appears to be cold and hungry, but the mother is nearly dead and can do nothing for it.

What are we to do?"

"I'm not sure, first though Amanda gets that doctor here as fast as you can and as quietly as you can. We will try to clean it up a little, Didn't you say you also knew a good and trustworthy cop? Well if you do we need him too, just try to hurry and be quiet about it as well."

"On it Steve, I have already talked to the doctor so he is on alert for whatever we need him to do."

"I know the same trooper she is talking about, I wish I had thought of him myself sooner, I'll get him right away," said Kerri. She left Amanda with Steve and Deanna and was gone less than an hour. She had instructed Her friend to use caution when approaching and perhaps hide his cars as well.

"Amanda and Deanna, could not leave the baby as it was. After all the girls had been through, they always kept an odd assortment of things in Steve's truck. First, they washed the new mother as much as was possible in this place. Also, they found a small stove, apparently to heat some soup or something while they took turns molesting her. The girl's name was Belinda, and she was happy someone was there to care for her baby. She thought if the four guys came back they would probably kill it. She felt that she would die anyway, with or without the baby.

"Steve this is Doctor King, and I brought him along as I felt we would need him. This other man is Captain Gregory McKnight he is with the troopers."

"Oh my Good suffering God, it looks like an extremely violent orgy here. When I call in forensics, they are going to blow their tops that we have been ahead of them and the evidence has been tampered with. What are you going to do with the baby? At least Kerri said something about a baby. I should be calling child welfare or someone to see to its care. What do you intend to do with it? I am sure it did not get up and walk away, as well as the fact that it will need food and clothing immediately. Come on we had better clear out of here before the guys come back. I'll keep a couple of my boys sort of lounging around, I already called in a report so they will have a heads up on our where abouts. A search warrant has been obtained and so we are ready for them. Can I get some sort of a message or statement from the mother?"

"Wish I could say yes, but she wouldn't be

able to tell you very much at this time. The next couple of hours will determine whether or not she lives or passes over. Thank you for your help Captain, I will be sure to keep you posted."

"Don't I know you from somewhere? You look awfully familiar. Wait I remember you're that Cop that they tried to pin a wrap on a year or so ago. I thought they proved it wasn't you, are you back with the force now?"

"I almost was, but then I met a ghost and the rest is history. "

"Yeah I hear ya, I met one before she was a ghost, and then she disappeared. I have been searching for her it seems as though forever. But then today when you sent for someone to help out here, there she was. A ghost sure, but it was her. We will have a lot to talk about after this case is solved and we can be alone. She cried, when she saw me, damn so did I. Imagine a grown man and a trooper at that crying like a kid would do. So what are you doing now, other than this I guess?"

"I have a sort of detective or private eye business now. But, don't laugh when I tell you. I run this strictly above board, but my crew is not what you could call average, they are mostly all ghosts. If someone told me this is what I would be doing a year ago, I would have driven them at gun point to see a head shrink.   It's a long story, after we get this settled come by my house and we can shoot some pool or just talk. Obviously, you can not only see them but talk to them too. I am told that is a rare gift, but I am also learning a lot of things I never knew before. Wait, I hear a couple of cars coming. I expected it to be a much longer wait than this. I can count 3 different men so far, but Kerri told us there were four. "

"What do you mean you just left her?"

" I had to get the hell out of here there was blood all over everything, and her yelling, what else could I do? "

" Well for one you could have untied her, so it wouldn't have looked as if she was being held for whatever reason. If anyone finds her, guess what it will do for our reputations. Hey what did you really do, she isn't here and neither is the kid."

"Well don't blame me, she was here and yelling her fool head off, when I left.   Where was Harold anyway? He should have been here too".

"We don't either of us know any more than

you do. But unless we find that broad we may be in a heap of shit. Look around while you are at it, and try wiping any signs that we were ever here away, If she was found, and all that yelling is what made someone come looking to see what was wrong, they could be back with the law."

Steve stepped into view just as the three men began to look around. "Hello gentlemen, was there something you were looking for?"

"Who the hell are you? We just thought we heard a loud noise in here so we thought we should check it out and see if it was an animal or something. Well as long as there doesn't seem to be anything wrong, we might as well leave," said George. He began backing toward the door and looked to see if the other men were coming too.

"I think maybe you boys might want to stay awhile," said another voice speaking softly. "There seems to be some interest in the goings-on here in this old barn. Would you boys know anything about it? The girl that we found had a lot to say before we rushed her to a hospital. She sort of named names as well as descriptions and many more things that might have been helpful here but the doctor said she was in no condition to talk anymore tonight.   He wasn't even sure if she would live until morning. So how about you three guys doing some talking?"

"We don't know nothing," said the one called Jason. "For all we know, it was all you two guys, what did this. So now you are trying to rope us in on your crime.   We don't know nothing, so we will just go on our way and you can't prove, we had anything to do with this girl or her baby either."

"Gee Captain Gregory, these boys have the idea there was a girl in here. I thought when you called us in on this case it was about a couple of reprobates jackin deer. They are claiming there was a woman with a baby,   where did they ever come up with that story?"

"You guys are just shooting at stars, we didn't say anything about a woman with a baby. So we will just leave now, and you can make up all your own stories. Now   if you will move aside, we will be leaving"

'I'm afraid we can't do that. As a matter of fact You three gentlemen are under arrest for rape, kidnaping, abuse, and a few more charges. Now you have the right to remain silent, anything you say may be held against you in a court of law, if you do not have an attorney one will be appointed for you.”

“Wait, where did you come up with this farce? First, you have to be a cop to make an arrest, next if this were real how do you two guys plan on holding three men?”

“Well to start with,” said Steve. “This gentleman is a Captain with the troopers. I am a private investigator, and we have both the girl in question and her baby. So you really don’t have any choice and as far as us holding you we just might have a few men standing by.”

“He’s right, let’s go we have a lot of paperwork to get done tonight. By the way you three guys might save us a little work if you each tell us your full names. We will have them all within an hour anyway but this would look better if people thought you were at least helpful.”

“Go to Hell cop, we’re not telling you anything, You’re just barkin’ at the moon.”

“Well, at least I offered, bring them out to the cars boys and take them downtown. Be careful the little guy has a mean mouth, but he runs at the sight of a little blood. Let’s see now the mouthy one would be Jason Barred, the one that hasn’t spoken yet is Calvin Boyles, George Avery, and the absent gentlemen would be Harold Orrin. We have them so far on kidnaping charges, rape, abuse, and peddling drugs, not to mention murder. So just come along nicely and we will let the courts decide who is guilty of what. By the way, I suppose you don't know anything about a girl named Kerri Kogan? She also went missing, and you should see her now. She lost a little weight, but after all, she has been through, she looks great I think," said Captain McKnight, gazing toward where Kerri was standing. She smiled back at him and then followed Steve and Deanna out. "Thanks for the names," whispered Gregory McKnight to Kerri. "Can I see you later, maybe at Steve and Deanna's place? It might be kind of late, by the time we finish up here though. We will have a thorough investigation into these three as well as fingerprinting these boys and this place, the forensic team will be out here for hours, so if that is too late or too early as this moves forwards, I will understand."

"Even in this form that I have become? I am after all a ghost now and I can't change back. Also, there are the facts of what was done to me, are you sure you can accept all of that. If you say yes to this, then I want you to know ghosts don't sleep and it would never be too late or too early either."

Chapter 3

Morning found a very tired but good-natured Trooper knocking on the door of Steve and Deanna's and asking for coffee.

"Well you look beat", observed Steve. "Come on in and have some coffee. Since so many ghosts didn't know they could eat or drink coffee, we have a large pot on at all hours.   We also have a large supply of coffee cakes, donuts, and pastries. My wife loves to cook, but I am always amazed by her, she even makes scones that are to die for. But I'm sure you didn't come here to talk to me. So I'll let Kerri know you are here."

"You don't have to call me, I am right beside you. Good Morning Gregory. You look tired, was it a long night?"

"That is putting it mildly. The fourth man was waiting for us, so I assume one of the first three got a chance to tip him off that we were coming for him. Would you believe he was an upright citizen with a wife and a daughter? He used them as a shield at first and then shot them and himself. So I guess I would say it has been quite a day's work. "

"Well then if you will follow me, I have a room here that is just right for what you really need. This way we can talk alone because I did not leave you for no reason, I couldn't help it." Gregory followed her to a small bedroom in the back of the house. Here she sat him down on the side of a bed, gently pushing him back until he was laying flat on his back. She began to talk to him quietly, and somehow soothingly. Within minutes, he was asleep. She managed to remove his jacket and tie without disturbing him and his shoes and socks as well. Then she sat down in a rocking chair and allowed him to sleep quietly for some time. When he roused up he felt more rested than he had been in years. But he was also appalled at himself for sleeping for so long instead of checking in at the office, say nothing of the fact he had been in a bed room alone with a young woman, and it was something he would never have done.

Kerri assured him there was nothing wrong by his being there with her alone.   "One of the things you don't understand is we have things we are able to do, sort of like magic.   I sort of lulled you to sleep as I could see you needed it. You just needed to relax. I'm sorry if I shouldn't have done that, but I was afraid you would drop from sheer exhaustion, and perhaps when you needed it the most you wouldn't have been able to get your second wind."

"No you didn't do anything wrong, I often sound grumpy like this when I first wake up; it depends on what had happened earlier or whatever case I was working on. Do you suppose I could have a cup of coffee? I sure could use one," he asked as he dressed his feet and looked around for his tie and jacket.

"No problem, come on and I'll even fix you some food if you would like it. By now Steve is working and the doctor is in checking on David."

"Who is David? Another ghost, or are their real people here too?"

"I'm sorry, but I'm new here too, so Steve will have to answer all of your questions. I'm just a ghost too, I'll find some real people for you to talk to."

"I'm sorry that didn't come out right. I just wanted to talk with you but I feel guilty being in a private room with a beautiful woman. I am not accustomed to being that bold or destroying a girl's reputation."

"Well, I think you are already too late for that. I would never have been in this disgusting shape if

I could have had any say in this. You said yesterday or was it today; it's hard to keep the days apart. That you had been searching for me, was it my parents or my best friend that noticed I was gone? How long had I been gone before anyone noticed?"

"No it wasn't them, I sort of got the feeling they hadn't noticed or even cared. Now I understand more what you had been going through. I'm sorry, But I had fallen in love with you, and hadn't had a chance to tell you because I couldn't find you."

Kerri began to cry softly and turned her back on him.

"No, please don't cry. Was it something I said?"

"No, it wasn't anything you said exactly. You see I have never heard those words before. I have never had anyone to love me." Kerri began to cry louder, "and now it is too late, she whimpered. I am dead and will never know the thrill of someone's arms around me, or feel his lips on mine. I will never know the joy of keeping house for someone or of having children. Gregory, how can you love me now? Even if I hadn't died, I could never have come with you as a woman that has been used.   Come on I will take you to Steve and he will try to put things in perspective for you." Kerri arose and went toward the door. Suddenly an arm flew out and Kerri was crushed up against a broad yet somehow tender chest. She found herself still crying but perhaps softer sobs.

"Damn it, Kerri, I don't care about that, I love you/ I don't know how this works or where it goes from here." He kissed her gently and held her tighter, as the kiss deepened".   He stepped back from her then shaking his head, "I'm sorry. I suppose you might have a case of police brutality. I know I felt you when I had my arms around you, and you were trembling. How could I feel it, just as I felt you kissing me back?"

"I don't know, I haven't been a ghost that long yet,"

"I think we had better join the others. Even if you are a ghost, I am afraid of my own feelings at this time. But now that I have found you I don't want to lose you again. No matter what it takes."

"Deanna, can we get some coffee, please? I think our Trooper needs at least that."

"Well you look more rested, what would you

like to go with that coffee?"

"Nothing thanks, but thank you for the coffee. This is a nice home you have here, and it feels comfortable. Sort of down-home and no matter what the problems you would be safe and made to feel welcome. But I need to make some phone calls and check-in at head quarts."

"One of Steve's rules, is coffee and a private phone line, so a person can make a call to anywhere and it will be private. We have several lines leading in here, and three of them are private. So be our guest and pick a phone, you may even take it to a different room if you like," said Deanna. "Oh yes there is an assortment of donuts and Danish-rolls if you should change your mind. There is a toaster and utensils if you wish only toast, jam, jelly we try to keep it all stocked many of us here only recently learned they can eat real food. So make yourself at home and eat what you want that little refrigerator is where you may find milk or cream if you like. Come on Kerri, Steve has some questions for you, and we can give Captain Mc Knight time to contact head quarts. The phone with the blue tape is private, but we change the colors sometimes."

Deanna took Kerri by the arm and led her to

an office where Steve was busy on the phone. Turning around he saw them and spoke a few words softly into the phone and hung up.

"So, now maybe someone can help clear your case up. What do you remember? I have here in the brief notes you left, that you were kidnaped, money not received so raped, and left tied up in an old shack. Is there anything you can add to this," asked Steve?

"No, except I didn't know anything about the kidnaping. I remember it was dark and I only heard their voices. I was there forever it seemed, and I didn't know what was happening. They came every so often to bring me food, like from McDonald's, or some such place. It was so long between these visits, and it seemed as though forever before I could have a drink of anything. Then one night they were all drunk and they decided to try some far-out sex exercises with me. I guess I passed out because I heard them talking off in a distance, telling someone that I would not be a burden anymore, and besides they had another girl all lined up. Then they were laughing, as they moved farther away.

I don't remember where I was or if I was even nude or dead. For a long while, I slept, but I was cold, so I guess that is what woke me up. It was quite dark so I still didn't know where I was, all I knew was I was very cold, and hungry. I managed to walk and it seemed like forever before I saw what appeared to be houses. I smelled food, but glancing down at my self I realized I was clothed but barely as my clothes had been torn and dirty, so I skirted the first couple of houses. I came to a place where people were eating, going around that building I found a box full of clothes. I assume they were for some sort of a charity drive. At least they appeared to be clean, a little large for me but warmer than what I was wearing. There were no shoes but they probably wouldn't have fit. I managed for several days not being seen and eating anything from scraps that had been thrown out from restaurants. Finally, I decided I must be dead as people didn't see me, and went about their business. I found some shoes that had been thrown out and they were only a little worn out, but sheer heaven to me. I managed to wash in a stream and saw how bad I looked. I have no idea where I was or how I got there, but I knew I had to get cleaner than I was, and that I couldn't stay the way I was forever. Then suddenly I heard screams and knew I had to help someone if I could just follow the noise. Walking is slow but sure and that is when I found Belinda, I wish it had been sooner. That is also when I met Amanda, she brought me here, so you could help. Deanna I want to thank you for the shower and clean clothes that actually fit. And shoes too, I will never again complain about my shoes or clothes. I am warm now, and I have finally found not only myself but also the man I have been in love with from the first time we met.

I am not sure what we can do about it as things stand but I'm willing to try anything."

Deanna looked across to Steve and shook her head slightly. She then asked   Kerri to follow her into the next room, and introduced her to Paula, "She is going thru much the same things, I think she can help you."

"David hasn't woke up in several hours, should I start worrying now or just keep waiting? Doctor Roberts said he was sleeping now but he keeps making weird noises. Sometimes it is as though he were somewhere else and talking to Steve, but then he is gone again and fighting."

"Just keep waiting is what the doctor said, so all we can do is wait. I want you to meet Kerri, she has very similar problems. I thought you could help her, work through some of yours as well as hers."

The two girls seemed to instinctively know what the other needed and was thinking. Deanna returned to the part of the house she felt the most comfortable in, that was where Steve was.

"Well, Deanna we seem to be finding more people than we know what to do with. What is being done about the baby and its mother?"

"I was just about to ask you the same thing. With the help from God, the baby is still alive and doing well. The mother is holding on by sheer willpower and we are not sure even yet as to her chances. She has asked to see you and the doctor says at this stage of things it can't hurt. I almost think it is too late, she seems to be crossing over. But look at how I was;   and at the way David is, sometimes here and then he is gone again. Is he alive really and in some sort of a coma or is he just fighting a losing game ?"

"We will worry about him later, right now let's check on Belinda. Also, there is a doctor by the name of King, even Paula says he is alright, and I think a real live doctor at this stage of the game might be just what we ordered right now. Between him and Doctor Roberts maybe we need to find a couple of nurses and we can have a medical degree or license or whatever is needed here, " he laughed. He went with Deanna to talk to Belinda. "Hello Belinda, do you know where you are or how you got here? Take your time I would rather you got well before you talk."

"No it is alright I need to talk to you. I don't know if I am going to live or die, but I need to think of my baby. Can you take her to my parents? I think they will understand and not hold it against the baby. I was due to start college in the spring, but Harold was mad because I didn't go out with him, so he and his pals grabbed me one night and took turns over and over until I just wanted to die. I guess I passed out because when I came to again I found myself in this ratty old house. They stuffed rags in my mouth so I wouldn't scream. They fed me something every so often, and I was always thirsty. It was my first time and I guess it is easier to get pregnant, whatever I did. I tried not to say anything but eventually, they could tell. I heard them talking about a ring where they take girls to old men for toys and babies are usually killed. I don't know anything else until I got here and cleaned up and fed. I wasn't judged, but my parents probably will. If they don't take little Ginny   in I will sign all the papers to put her up for adoption."

"We'll take care of your baby, no matter what

happens. Give us your full name and an address for your house, and we will approach it as carefully as we can. Is there anything special that can identify us to them so they won't think we are just trying to pawn a baby on them to raise? Perhaps a birth mark or some small thing only a parent would know about?"

"I have a strawberry mark on my heel and my mother has one as well. They aren't really bad parents just a little strict. They would rather think I was dead than to find I had been raped over and over. A good girl would think first of her reputation and her parent's place in society, rather than allow themselves to be used and not at least have tried to kill herself. I suppose I am just weak I couldn't kill myself; especially after I knew about Ginny. Do you think she will be able to keep her name?"

"I don't see why not," murmured Deanna. "We will wait a couple of days so we can determine how you are and we have two doctors here to care for you and the baby."

Just then Paula burst through the door to let both doctors and Steve know that David was alive and trying to get up. They all rushed in to see David sitting up in bed and attempting to get his clothes.

"I have to go," he said. "I am already late for an appointment, why did you let me sleep so long, Paula? Who are these people, am I that weird looking?"

"No," said Doctor King. "But you seem to be able to get up alone, so go ahead. It is just that you have been sick for quite awhile, and we didn't think you were strong enough yet. That is a good sign that you think you are now ready. Stand up slowly and we will be here if you feel weak."

"I'm not an invalid yet, so just step aside and I will be out of here. I will admit to feeling a little dizzy tho."

"Oh dear he is walking funny and now he seems to be having seizures of some sort. You have been friends since childhood, has he ever gone through this before that you know of?"

"No, not that I ever knew about."

"If it was epilepsy there should have been some early signs of spells. He seems to be going through violent muscle contractions usually caused by epilepsy. But other things such as very low blood sugar levels, high fever, or a stroke. We need to get Lab tests or images, then we will know if it was brought on by his blood sugar levels or even a stroke. But at times it can easily be cured as soon as the cause is found or it can possibly be critical or even be life-threatening. If I had been his doctor for awhile now I would have labeled this as a Grand Mal Seizure.

" What do we do", asked Doctor Roberts? "Is it possible for us to just walk in put him in the examining room and then take x-rays etc?"

"No I'm not sure what we will do about it yet, I think we need to plan this very carefully; hey where did he go? I am sure he could not have just walked out of here on his own."

Chapter 4

"You said the magic words, and there was no way of stopping a determined ghost. When you said it could be critical even life-threatening, that was all she needed to hear. My guess is she got another of the ghostly two and he is even now being hooked up ready for x-rays etc, So perhaps we had better hurry before they have him hooked up to a life support unit."

"How did they get him in without being seen? Suppose someone did see them, and the law is there waiting for us, no I guess I mean me because no one can see you or hear you. To think I even chose this profession. I'll lose my license, I'll go to jail. I suppose I can plead my own case 'I'm innocent, it was the ghost that did it'. Oh well, it's too late to worry about it now, let's go. Oh yes, you are planning to fly along, aren't you?   You have to come with me, it's as much your fault as it is mine. Excuse me Judge but my, friend here can tell you all that

happened. What do you mean you can't see him or hear him either? Why do you feel as if I need a shrink?"

"Doc you are a funny man.   I don't think

you will be arrested, besides the girls won't let you down. They are just worried about David, especially Paula."

When they arrived at the hospital everything seemed to be quiet and peaceful. Doctor King walked toward the nurse's station, but no one was there, so he began to look around for the x-ray room. This was not the hospital where he normally worked so he was not sure where anything was. He managed to locate the right room and found the girls with David. Just as Doctor Roberts said they had him in a hospital gown and he was hooked up to an IV. Looking around the room he finally saw a shadow of sorts indicating the place where he assumed the girls were standing.

"Okay girls, I'm not sure how you have managed this, but let's get those x-rays before someone comes looking to see what is going on, Which one of you knew how to hook up an IV? Everything appears to be working right, so far."

"I was studying to be a nurse before I got married," said Paula. "So it sort of came in handy, I also did blood work on him a few days ago at the house and took it down with a factious name, and I have kept track of his blood pressure. It has been a little high lately.   Do you think that could have been what led to these violent muscle spasms ?”

“It is possible that it at least contributed to it. Now that we have gotten these tests done, we need to get him back out of here without being seen, and leaving everything as we found it.”

“Oh no, what do we do now? Doctor Roberts, you have to know what to do.”

“What do you mean Paula? What is happening that I don’t know about, David looks the same to me. How are we getting him out of here? Could one of you help me lift him into this wheelchair, cover him up well so maybe no one will notice us.”

“Doctor King, he isn’t here right now.”

“Not here? Of course, he’s here we have to get him out of here fast.”

“Perhaps you had better get his heart rate fast, as in right NOW/”

“We don’t have time for this, we must move him right now before we get caught running tests here.”

“Okay it is your patient, lets go. Doctor

Roberts, you explain to him, we will get him home and in a bed."

"Hey, who the h–ll is in charge around here? You said a month or so ago that we had to wait, well I have waited long enough. Now I want to see the top dog in this operation. Hey/ is anyone listening to me or not, what do I have to do to get some attention around here?"

"First you do not need to yell, and second we do not allow any profanity in this house. From time to time we have small children here as well as the fact our own daughter is here. Now please state your name and tell us briefly why you are here."

"What I have to say is for your boss, that way I don't chew my cabbage twice. I ain't no kid that has to talk nice cause it might hurt somebody with delicate ears. A little damn and shit don't hurt no body. So rather than standing there with your finger up your ass go find your boss. I ain't got all day to be farting around with some damn broad."

"I'm also sorry sir but I will not tell anyone you are here because you aren't as far as I am concerned. I have already told you the rules about swearing, obviously, you either do not hear or you are too stupid to follow the rules. So for the last time may I have your name and briefly the problem that needs immediate attention."

"Clean your ears out bitch, I already told you what I have to say is to a man. Not some mollycoddling dame that is probably only here to be some rich guy's toy."

"Did I or did I not just hear someone call my wife a female dog in heat? Also as I am sure you have been told about swearing on the premises. In fact, I heard you told more than once about your language. Now you can either tell me what you want and in a civil tongue or leave the choice is yours to make."

"I can't help that child if you don't f–king listen to me. So no more damn swearing."

"Already I should toss you out on your but, however since there is a child involved; I feel we should start getting as much information. Now, what is your name?"

"My name is Herbie Green, and I work for Mr. Harrison, but these other dudes are trying to take over, they won't of course because my boss is too smart for that."

"Well, then Herbert why are you here? You

mentioned a child, what is wrong with this child? Where is this child?"

"I already told that broad the name is Herbie, not Herbert. The kid is somewhere out in those woods alone. The new guys were trying to put the squeeze on Mr. Harrison, but he is too smart for them. He nabbed the kid before those other guys could, but then they started to argue and the one they called Roscoe started to show off what a good shot he was, and my boss called me in on this guy. We was shooting at targets and the other guy slipped in the mud and shot me by accident. I'll bet my boss was mad, cuz he always took good care of me. But everyone forgot the kid, and I couldn't tell them anything cuz I was dead."

"Well then Mr. Herbie, why didn't you do anything to help the child on your own?"

"What the f– oh yeah language, sorry. I have no idea how this stuff works, know what I mean? I never been dead before. I thought because the way I've lived and all I would be going where it was really hot. But so far it ain't bad, if anything it's cold, I'll sure be glad when summer gets here. Now all I can tell you is the kid is in an old refrigerator somewhere out that old road that was abandoned a couple of years ago because of the swamp always flooding it.”

“How long has the child been in there? Can you lead us there?”

“I’m going with you,” said Deanna. “I will take one of the girls with us also some clean dry clothes.   Is this a boy or a girl, how old you think it is”

“Hey this ain’t no place for a dame, besides it could be dangerous, you stay here and make some cookies or whatever it is you dames do, this is man's work.”

“Now wait a minute,”

Steve winked at Deanna and gave her a little nod. “We won’t be very long, so just follow behind us,” whispered Steve over Herbie’s shoulder. They drove out to a place that Herbie indicated and was almost too late, as there was a van with several girls in it.

“Are these friends of yours,” asked Steve with a straight face? “Should I get out and introduce myself,” he asked?

“No, those are the men from the other gang, or I mean side. That one over there is the one that shot me by mistake. But those are some of the broads they have been fighting over."

"Is it possible that they should not be referred to as broads? For all you know they may be very nice girls from a good neighborhood with nice families."

"Yeah I suppose, but then why do they want them so bad they are fighting over them."

"Awehh come on Jake let's get these dames delivered. You know the boss is going to be mad as it is because we are taking so long. I don't care what you think that kid would bring, if we don't make delivery soon he'll have us shot or whatever it takes to get rid of us just like he did with old Herbie.   Ha, ha, old Herbie never knew what hit him. He thought I shot him by accident, but the truth of it was Mr. Harrison wanted to get rid of the jerk. So we had a fake shooting contest so I accidentally shot him. I'll never forget the surprised look on his face. He thought it was an accident but Harrison was glad it went so well. It looked better to the other side that he was willing to get rid of his own man and he could blame Herbie for the fake double-cross too."

"So, said Steve in a whisper, your boss set you

up, but you think he'd a great guy that always looks out for you, huh?"

"Nah, I don't believe that, he's just trying to make me mad enough so he can start a fight."

"Really, but you're already dead so how can he start a fight with a corpse? You wait here and stay dead, I'll try it my way. Deanna you and Amanda be careful getting those girls out. That one girl must be the kid's mother try to quiet her down and see if she knows where the child is." Walking slowly through the trees and brush they had been using for cover, Steve approached the front of the van and began to talk as if he had been there all the time and part of the conversation.

"Hello boys, nice night for a coon hunt, what ya think? Oh were you leaving? But I just got here, what's your hurry? Better be quiet and tell your wife to stop yelling like that, there are cops all around us and they will find us sure as anything. Some guys are shanghaiing young girls and selling them for some prostitute ring. I wouldn't want to be the guys when they catch them. Seems that one of the girls was a cop's daughter, wow when those guys get caught."

"Shoot him don't just stand there looking at

him. We've got to split and don't have time for this guy."

"But do you see who is standing beside him? That's Herbie but it can't be. But I would stake my life on it that is him. Hell, I am staking my life on it, let's go."

"That Van won't start unless you have these," said Deanna holding up spark plugs and a distributer cap.

"Hey you ain't one of our girls, but you would sure help us fill an empty spot in our van."

"Oh I think the van has lots of room now anyway." Steve backed away from the two men as they seemed more interested in Deanna. Then ducking around the van and coming up behind the two men with guns he knocked the arm of one man up in the air and spun around kicking just under the belt line of the other man. Steve swung on the first man making sure he dropped the gun and then sort of threw the first man at the second man. Deanna grabbed for both guns and managed to get one of them Amanda had stopped herding the girls to a safe place and came back invisible, "Are you boys still playing? Well then shoot me, I'm right here in front of you, whoops not there over here she said as she dodged around. Okay times up, now be nice little boys and get in your van and go away. Oh that's right it won't start. Well Steve maybe we should just tie them up and leave them here. Let's tie them to a tree then we can use the van for the girls. I just called your friend the chief John Zophy. He has a crew on his way here with all the necessary papers and is about to make a big arrest. He and his men already know all about the king pins in this outfit and has them already in custody."

"Hey I never knew no broads, excuse me, women smart enough to help like this. You br– I mean ladies sure were a big help and even sent for the law without being told to do it. Wow, but how did you know what to do to fix their van so it wouldn't run. Even I wouldn't have known that. "

"Hey there Steve what are you doing? Trying to do everything by yourself? I thought that when the going got tough and all that stuff. While you and this potato head were here mashing all the girls this bozo was coming at you with a gun and he had backup too. I just sort of fouled up their plans, hope you don't mind."

"David, how did you find us? What are you doing here, I thought they had you at the hospital running tests or something. But no as usual you are beside me cleaning up my mistakes. Did you happen to see John Zophy out there on your way in?"

"No but he didn't see me either. Want me to find him or just relieve you of your packages?"

"What I want is to find a child they have put in a refrigerator someplace. But yes it will help if you tell John where we are, although he has got to be busy with the mess he found out here himself. Damn, oops sorry Deanna, but that man is a good cop. Wish we had a hundred more just like him, no more crime anywhere close to us. Between him and McKnight of the troopers what a team we would have made. But enough talking go get Jimmy and I'll keep looking for the kid."

"I'm already here Steve, why didn't you call me sooner?"

"I would have if I had known what was going on. All we heard was there was a child of undetermined age or sex. This guy came in cussing a blue streak and saying we had to find the kid. He said he was shot by accident, so he couldn't go to the law ."

"Well he looks alright to me, maybe a little

under the weather but not really dead yet."

"How can he see me? I never seen no ghosts. Is he like you know clair violet or something."

"Not that I ever knew about he isn't clairvoyant, but you never know. The truth is we feel that where ever your body is you are still alive. But that doesn't mean we can save you, but as soon as we find that kid we will try and locate your body and see what we can do."

"Steve, over here, I think I can hear someone or something coming from that old freezer in that pile of junk."

Steve and the Deanna walked quickly toward the junk pile, walking carefully over all of the old motors and garbage through what once appeared to be a dump; they found what David was pointing to. It was thrown down and there were things on top of it. "How could someone have even gotten to it and put someone in it and covered it with more garbage? This does not seem right, David I think you are hearing things."

"I think you could be right Steve, this looks to be the right size to put someone in." Calling to a couple of his men to help dig this freezer out they quickly removed some boxes and a couple of tires to get to the door.

"I think," said Jimmy. "This stuff was thrown on top to throw off anyone looking. Joe," he shouted to one of his men," get me a crow bar anything that will get this door off from here, they seem to have locked it in case we found it."

With-in a short time they managed to tear the door off and rescue the small boy.   He was all out of breath from crying and being inside as well.

"Steve did you notice this," asked James? "They took time to put a small tube in side so he had some air at least. We never would have noticed it if we hadn't demolished the door."

Deanna grabbed the child and held him tightly until his crying stopped and he was reasonably calm.

"I want mama," he sobbed. "Momma, momma ."

"I'm here baby, momma is right here." She grasped the little boy tightly and began to croon to him softly.

"This is one of the girls they were taking for their prostitute ring. We have all the girls safely away from there do you need them any more Jim?"

"Will you be taking them to your place? Then if there are any questions I'll know where to find them."

" All right gang, let's get these girls back to the house, I don't imagine any of them have had any food or rest."

"Just a minute what about me," asked Herbie? "After all if I am still alive, I want to know it."

We have no idea where your body is. Do you remember where you were when your boss was being careful to take care of you?"

"I think I remember so let's go."

"Well if you don't need me, I guess maybe I'll go back too. I'm not sure where I left my body either."

"I'll come with you, said Deanna the girls do need to get out of this weather. It looks as if it is going to rain, it might be a tight fit but we'll manage."

" No you don't have to do that I'll just be a minute putting these plugs back and the distributor cap on as well."

"I forgot we have the van, but David we always carry a spare set of plugs and sometimes a distributor cap as well. We didn't take the ones from the van but they didn't know that. So all we have to do is start the van and drive home."

"How come Steve gets all the breaks, if only I had found you first. I would sure have given Steve a run fo his money."

"Yes but then you never would have met Paula."

"That's right I wouldn't have met Paula. Deanna do you think this place I am in now will make it easier for Paula and me?"

"I don't really know David. You're not really dead so you aren't a ghost, but you aren't really alive either. It will take someone with more smarts than me to answer that question. Meanwhile, let's go home, that's where the rest of you can be found."

"How far is it from here," asked Steve. "We can use my truck as long as the girls and David are taking the van."

"I'm not sure, many things are mixed up for me lately. I thought the kid was in a refrigerator and it turned out to be a freezer. The kid would have died just by that mistake alone. I will admit, I put him in there so those guys wouldn't find him. Then I sort of threw things on top of the freezer trying to make it look as if no one had been in there. Now I see that I nearly killed him too. Maybe it is better that I really am dead because I've done a lot of things wrong in my life. I guess I never thought I was doing wrong, I was just following orders. I never started thinking about things until lately, I deserve to be dead."

Steve just began driving, he went where Chief Zophy told him they had arrested the men connected with this case. He stopped the truck and got out, calling to Herbie. "Well does any of this look familiar to you?"

"Yeah, we was standing right over there," he answered. Pointing to a place just out of sight of the road. "There," he said pointing again. "That's my body, I sure look bad don't I?"

Chapter 5

"Well I don't think you look as if you are going to a party." Talking into his phone, he asked Chief Zophy if he had heard everything. He was on his way and would be there within the hour. He had to drop the rest of his scum baggage to jail and told his superintendent he would be back to make out his reports.

Steve had told Deanna about where he would be and ask her to send Doctor Roberts out to him. Within minutes Dr. Roberts was there and examining the body. "He's lost a lot of blood but since he has not moved far and there has been a chill factor involved the rain was really working in their favor. Normally we wouldn't consider that a good thing, but it has helped in this case. However he needs to be out of this weather now if we are going to save his life, There are still a lot of factors to take into him living or dying. It appears that the big guy upstairs seems to think he might be worth saving. This act of trying to save the child no matter what the circumstances might be has gone a long way in God's eyes. I'll take him back to the house, you hurry up and get back as well."

"Hey Herbie remember me," asked a voice from somewhere? "You probably don't remember your boss told you to waste me, but you shot me in the shoulder and smeared the blood to look like I had been shot in the chest. You told your boss you were just making sure I was dead. Then you whispered to me to get a doctor for that shoulder wound and said I should live. I did too for a couple of years met a nice girl, got married had two kids, but then one night while I was driving in a snow storm I cracked up and died. But thanks to you I went straight and had a good life for awhile. There are others, you couldn't save us all but a few of us made it thanks to you."

"Well it looks as if you are going to live after all, so how about you going straight."

Several months went by with no major problems. Summer came and Steve and Deanna had a beautiful wedding. Krista passed her grade with flying colors. Except for some minor cases entirely within Steve's capability, he managed to solve each of them without any major problems. He had been in to check on David daily and did not notice any change. He was beginning to worry and even Paula was worried.

"I think I would know if he crossed over and became a full-fledged ghost. But this is so hard not knowing what to expect," said Paula.

David suddenly sat up and looked around, "What are we doing today? Has the snow finely gone?"

"It sure has, and now we are having a hot dry spell. You slept through the slow sluggish spring and halfway into Summer."

"I wouldn't have woke up now except for those kids crying. Are you raising kids now? If you are then why are they crying so hard."

"No we only have Krista here and Belinda's baby. But no one is crying."

"No don't hit her, she didn't do anything wrong. You can't keep taking her food away, and then beating her as well." David was not looking toward either Steve or Paula, he appeared to be in almost a trance.

"I don't think he even knows where he is, he is seeing someone or something and it has him greatly disturbed.   I don't know if I should try to wake him up or just leave him. I think we will have to stay with him though or he could get hurt."

"Steve should we call Dr. Roberts, or just wait and see what will happen?"

"Damn, I feel terrible Steve. Say, did we go out last night?"

"David we have got to get another doctor in or find out what is wrong. You seem to go into a sort of trance or something and don't seem to know where you are. You sat here on the edge of the bed but not really there anymore. You are seeing things that aren't around us and we can't help you because we don't know where you are or who you are seeing. You seem to be somewhere and can see children that are being abused. Can you tell us anything or at least what to do to help you."

"No I don't know where I am, but children are being made to work like slaves and then punished when it isn't done fast enough or done good enough. Then I can see and sometimes hear these children, crying from the whippings they get and no food for them either. They are dressed in rags and no shoes, they are also dirty, and most of them sleep on cold floors with only a thin blanket to cover up with. Am I just going crazy myself or is this happening somewhere?"

"Well my friend if you find that out, remember I am here if you need me."

"I love you, Paula, I'm sorry to be putting you through all of this. I think I'm a little tired, when I wake up we will talk."

"And just like that, he's asleep again. He isn't eating but he doesn't seem to be losing weight."

"I'll be in the other room if you need me. We have finally persuaded Belinda's parents to come here to talk about her disappearance, we were waiting for her to be a little stronger."

"I may drop-in, no not really I meant float in. I am sort of curious how parents can hold it against their daughter that she didn't kill herself when she was raped and to allow herself to get pregnant by one of them and not kill the baby too. This I have got to see, and so does Amanda, and Kerri."

"True enough, the doctor said she was well enough to take all that gets dished out. I'm not even sure Krista should hear any of this either. But on the other hand, she has been exposed to so much, maybe in a way it could be beneficial to her so she knows there are many different people in the world and they aren't all completely bad."

"What does her mother think about her listening to the happenings that will be going on?"

"She isn't too keen on the idea but thinks now she is seeing how a good girl can be thrown down, as if she herself were guilty. She also thinks if she had not been killed, what sort of life would it have been for her daughter. Or if it hadn't been for us that found her, would she have wound up in the roll of a hooker too? This would not have been her choice either, so does that make her bad for not killing herself when she was eight or ten? I'll let you know when they get here. By the way, I keep forgetting Deanna and I, want to get some of those walkie-talkies gadgets to put in every room so in case of any emergencies we can reach someone faster."

"Daddy, come quickly;" called Krista.   She was gasping for air and crying all at the same time.

Deanna reached her first, and pulled her as close; as she tried to calm her down enough to understand what she was saying. Amanda came at a dead run with a cold wet wash cloth in her hand. She handed the cloth to Deanna, who began to slowly wash her face and smooth her hair back from her face.

Steve also came on a run with Paula right behind him. "I'm here Poppet, what is wrong ?"

"That man scared me. He told me that my mother was very sick and needed to see me right away. But when I laughed at him, he grabbed me and tried to pull me in the van. I kicked him really hard and then hit him very hard like you told me to. When he yelled and let go I ran as fast as I could and came here. But I think he picked up Rose, she was walking home with me. I did what you told me to and very calmly remembered his license plate number and it was a blue car but I don't remember what kind it was, sorry."

"You did everything right poppet, I'll go and tell the police. We'll find out about Rose too, you will have probably saved her life. Deanna look out and see if the van is still out there."

"Don't worry Steve, No body hurts my daughter, or even scares her. The van is sitting around the corner steam pouring out from under the hood and Rose is now safe too. They are so busy arguing as to who caused the car trouble, they didn't even notice. Rose is coming here right now to check on Krista. Oh yes I called Gregory McKnight too and told him what was going on. In fact you can see the lights flashing now."

"Thanks Amanda, you gals always do great jobs. Let Kerri know he's out there as well. Krista and I are going for a walk so maybe they will understand even the kids around here are protected, Come on Rose, you did good too. Let's go tell the policeman out there what these guys were trying to do, so maybe some other kid will know what to do too."

A short time later a car pulled up and a man and his wife got out and started for the door when they saw the police car parked in the side driveway.

"Come on Isaac, we don't want to go in here, they apparently are having trouble with the law.   Our standing in the community will drop for sure, to think our daughter is somehow connected to these people. Come quickly," she said "We don't want anyone seeing us that may recognize us. It would be just ghastly if our friends thought we were here. I always thought this was a better part of town, but I can see now that it isn't. I think when we get home I will call Deloris Jefferies and get a partition up to have people like that thrown out of our neighborhood."

"You may go if you desire, but I am going to see to MY daughter first. If you want my opinion I'm glad she didn't kill herself. It took guts (Yes I said GUTS) to go through what she must have gone through and still lived to tell about it. Now if you wish to leave, go ahead, but it is my car and it isn't leaving so have a nice walk." He then proceeded to walk up to the front door and ring the bell.

He was greeted by a man in a suit, who asked if he was expected.

"Yes we are the parents of Belinda Robbins, may we come in?" Sheila had followed her husband to the door but held back at the sight of the door man. 'See" she whispered to her husband," That's probably a body guard, I understand they have that kind of people guarding them from other gangs."

Hearing this, her husband merely smiled and went in. Sheila followed slowly, looking all around as she entered.

Steve, upon hearing voices, came out to greet them. He shook hands with Mr. Isaac Robbins. "Well hello, I am glad we have finally gotten to meet you. Won't you come into the living room. We can sit and get better acquainted. Would you care for something to drink? We have coffee at all times, but with all of this heat we have lemonade, a variety of fruit juices or ice tea. I would offer you something a little stronger but my wife does not allow alcoholic beverages in our home. I hope seeing the police car out front didn't frighten you Mrs. Robbins, but there are a   few inscrutable people in the world. Someone just tried to kidnap our daughter and another young girl as well. Fortunately, my daughter was able to break away and told the police in time to also save her friend. I have always taught her what to do and to remember the color of the car and the plate number, she did so well, that the suspects were apprehended with minutes. I sound as if I am bragging, I am, not bad for a nine-year-old, isn't it? I assume you have come to see Belinda, and we will let her come out and talk to you. She is still very weak from all the torture she has been through. So I wish to press upon you I will not allow anyone to see her, if it is merely to cause her more grief than she has already suffered through. There will be no recriminations whatsoever from either parent. She can come and go as she sees fit, but her doctor feels she must have a good deal more time before she can feel safe again. Also because of what she has suffered she may never recover completely.   But with love and care, we are praying for her complete recovery."

Steve rose from his seat and went to a door in the other side of the room and beckoned for

Belinda. She came in wearing a smile and showing all the love she had saved for this time, Her father quickly arose and crossed the room in two steps to clasp her tightly. "Oh my darling, my poor little girl, if we had only known we would have scoured the earth looking for you."

Belinda stepped back from her father with tears in her eyes. "How long did you look, Father? I was there so close and thought that any minute you would be there to rescue me. But time went on, with no one looking or even caring where I was. Not even caring if I was alive or dead, as long as it didn't upset Mothers standing in the community. I managed to have a baby in spite of being tied no way of cleaning myself or getting a drink if I was thirsty. Wishing I was dead because it would make all of the hurt go away. I was hungry really bad hungry, wolfing down anything I was given. Then I realized I was pregnant and I wouldn't tell them or they would have killed it, that would have made you happy mother. Finally, I could hide it no longer, and I could hear them plotting how to get rid of me, but it must be so no one knows. Do you know our neighbor, the Avery's or the really nice house with a lovely couple the Orrins and they have a little girl? That is who at least two of those nice people were mother. I understand that when he learned I had been rescued he shot his wife and daughter and then himself. I have named and described all of them. There was another girl before me, but they killed her. Now, mother and dad what do you think? I went to the best schools I was a straight-A student and was looking forwards to college, but what am I now. Will you be proud of me and take me home to see all of your friends? I don't hear either of you cheering now. Would you like to see your granddaughter, or is she bad too because she didn't stop breathing, worse it is almost impossible to determine which one was the father. I can have blood work done, but does that make any difference?

Belinda turned and left the room. Her mother was sitting stiff and staring straight ahead. "See what I told you, Isaac? We can not allow that person back in our home. We will either tell people that she was found dead, a hit and run. Or that she has been in Paris or somewhere and has decided to stay."

"Sheila, do you even hear yourself? She is our daughter, and you would turn your back on her because of circumstances beyond her own control?

"But Isaac, what will our friends say? And just look at her, she looks so sickly and even her hair and nails, not to mention her clothes."

"Well Sheila, I have only one thing to say to you, and it has been building for a long time now. I will wait until tomorrow for you to find another place to live, but I am going to divorce you. I should have done it years ago, as you gained in Prominence, you fell farther away from a wife or mother. I had hoped you would change, but you have only gotten worse. I will give you an allowance much smaller than what you are spending now, but an adequate amount for you to live comfortably. There will be no fighting over anything, The house and all of the furnishings belong to me, but I will have them listed on the block by this time tomorrow. Anything really you want I will consider but my lawyer will have the final say.   If you do not want to see our grand daughter than you may leave either wait and I will give you a ride to the house or call a taxi."

Belinda came back in the room looking from her mother to her father. Her father was smiling and went immediately toward the baby that Belinda was holding. "This is Ginny, your granddaughter."

"What a beautiful child she is and all smiles. Her hair is like yours and your mother's, all curls.

Belinda, I will gladly take you and Ginny back home. However, I do not know where that will be. Your mother and I have reached an understanding of sorts, and we are getting a divorce. I will be selling the house, and do not know where I will be yet. I am proud of you especially after all that you have endured and still managed to stay alive. I am going now, may I come back and visit until I have a permanent address for you?"

"Yes, of course, I am sad about this, but I understand. Mother, will you at least look at the baby?"

"Of course not, just look what you and that kid have done. Now I don't even have a home, nor will I ever be able to look my friends in the eye."

"That was not necessary Sheila, you are purposely striking back at anyone rather than admit it was your own fault. I have said nothing for years as you gained in popularity, you lost the love of your family. I loved you Sheila but a man can only take so much. Come on we will discuss this in the car alone. Now that we are alone, I want to ask you a very important question. If you feel that I am asking too late, remember this. I loved you from the first moment I saw you and the way you tipped your head up and smiled at me. You didn't want me to know what kind of girl you were so you began with a story and all you have had to endure living on the wrong of the tracks. Your father was a drunken lout that went around with dirt under his nails and rarely wore a clean shirt. The truth was he worked in a coal mine and rarely drank. He also wanted nicer things for both you and your mother so in his spare time, he worked at the butcher's shoveling guts and bones. It wasn't a white color job but it was honest work and paid him a decent wage. He died at a young age, and your mama sewed dresses for the ladies in town. But you learned while in your teens, that a pretty good deal of money could be had being nice to all the old lecherous men, and thus you came to me wanting me to pay you like the other men did. Big mistake because I fell in love with you and wanted to give you everything the rest of your friends only talked about. At first it was a good life, wasn't it? But then you felt you needed more and deserved more. I knew about all of your little flings but hoped you would settle down. Then it began with you putting on airs, trying to look the way you thought a prim and proper lady should act. Truth now Sheila, who is Belinda's father?"

"Why the way you carry on, one would think I was a scarlet woman. She belongs to you of course. Isaac how can you even think such a thing.

All those things you said about my family they just weren't true."

"Don't start that baby talk with me or that southern drawl either. You have learned to talk that way to perfection. I have already had the test results done some years ago, so I know who the father is. But I hoped you would tell me on your own, or is it possible there were so many you aren't even sure who it is."

Sheila began to cry, and then when Isaac ignored her, her tears became louder. "Oh Isaac how can you be so horrid to me? You know I love you and it has been you for all these years."

"Those are called crocodile tears, as phony as you are. I might have forgiven you no matter what, but to stand there and not see that baby or your own flesh and blood daughter, trying to make it seem as if she has done something wrong. That is the last straw on the camel's back, and it is now broken. Another thing, my lawyer already has most of the story on you, so there will be no arguments, Erik Logan and I have discussed the parentage of Belinda. Is that a surprised look on your face? Did you think I would believe all the stories you have used and then just as casually walk away? Where would you like me to drop you tonight? One of your gentlemen friends perhaps? You may come over tomorrow to get your clothes, and I suggest you bring a lawyer or someone you can trust. I will arrange a time you may come and I will have a legal representative there as well. If you had shown the small bit of affection toward Belinda or her daughter, I would have forgiven you completely. You do not ever have to see Belinda again after all it might cloud your name in society. Erik and I have agreed that I will be her full-time parent, One good thing that has come of this, Erik and I are closer friends now and he has quit drinking, he also told his wife Rose about it. She has forgiven him as long as he stays on the wagon." Isaac drove the rest of the way in silence, stopping once only long enough to get gas then he took Sheila back to her mother's house and left as soon as she got out of the car. He honked and waved at his mother-in-law, but kept driving without a backward glance. He made good time going home, the song on the radio was 'cowboys don't cry, well maybe they don't but it was hard-driving as he wept like a baby the rest of the way home.

The sale of the house went smoothly and then they had an auction for the rest of the household things' Belinda was there helping her dad with everything. She didn't understand it all and felt at first that it was her fault. She was old enough to know a few things, so in as delicate a way as was possible he told her about her mother. He left out a lot of it, and she got to meet Erik and his wife, they had been unable to have children of their own and were ecstatic when Belinda ask them to please be the Godparents for little Ginny. Belinda wanted to finish school as she had planned before her nightmare, so she took night classes and continued on in school. From time to time she still had nightmares but overall she was doing fine. Her mother came to the school one day asking for her forgiveness and Belinda forgave her. But still, she never ask to see little Ginny. Her father told her that she must be patient with her, he was sure that one day she would come around.

Chapter 6

Steve went in to check on David and found him sitting up at the table with Paula and a large plate of food in front of him.

"Welcome to the world of the living David. You look great, how do you feel?"

"I am fine why shouldn't I be? I have had all of this pampering from this young woman here, and there is a little girl that brought me food and cookies. I don't believe I got your name sir, is this how all of your patients are treated?"

Steve looked at Paula who merely gave a slight nod of her head. Then spread her hands out in askance.

Steve nodded again and whispered he would be outside and needed to see her.

"Is this a real reaction, or is he just kidding?"

"Your guess is as good as mine. He woke up and ask what time it was, then got dressed and ask for some coffee. This is the first he has been awake since he said there were children needing help as they were being made to work in terrible conditions, having food withheld and being beaten as well. He hasn't mentioned them again and has not even spoken of anything concrete but he seems to think he is in a nursing home or something similar."

"Where did you go, Lady could I please have some more coffee?"

"A few minutes ago he called me Paula, but now I'm hey lady. I don't even know what to say back to him. Are you coming back in or waiting for the doctor?"

"The doctor is here, I just saw him come in, so let's go back in and see what he has to say this time." Steve went back in and Paula followed with more coffee.

"Dad, can I tell Uncle David about the people that tried to catch me and Rose? Or will it be too much for him right now?"

"That might even help him right now. Yes by all means go in and tell Uncle David, he has been having bad dreams and this might clarify things for him."

"Hello Uncle David, was it you in a sort of

dream that helped Me and Rose get away from those men in the van a while ago? I was crying so hard but I ran and then one of mama's friends made them stop driving long enough to get Rose out too."

"What's this? Who are you, little girl? But I am glad you and your friend Rose, got away safely. Oh, thank you for the coffee Miss."

"Oh Uncle David you are so funny, you just called Paula, Miss and you know her name. But how come you just called me little girl? Have you forgotten me, you told me you never would forget."

Steve, feeling bad for Krista, tried to explain about David. "He is still very sick and sometimes he forgets who he is too, but as long as we have patience then we think he will be his old self again. The Doctor said it might be very good for him to see you because you have been the one person he seemed to remember. Right now it seems to be on and off, he was talking to Paula and all was well but then he lost touch again. I wish I could explain it better for you so you could understand. But mostly I don't understand either."

" Steve, where are you? Have you been taking

these cases by yourself, trying to make a name for your self huh?   Well old buddy you will not get away with that, I'm here beside you until you bite the radish. If you go first, just remember   I will be here too. Wait do you hear those kids again, we have to find them before it is too late. One of them died this morning and now they are trying to figure out where to put the body. We have got to get in there and stop this. I think it can be termed murder, but I would rather find them and rescue them, as slowly watch each of them die."

"Well Poppet, he is gone again. He doesn't even know where this place is, but he can see it. Wait a minute I might have thought of a solution to finding them. David, I'm right here beside you but I'm not sure how we got here. Did you recognize any landmarks so I can direct the police here?"

"Steve, you are the one who always does that. But let me look around for a minute or so. We turned down beaver road and then went toward the old ranger station, that's where we parked your truck. Now we are walking back into some deep woods, there is a light up ahead this is near the old fish hatchery. But why would they hide someone here? Have you called the police yet?"

"Yes but Gregory McKnight, needs to have a

reason to go charging in on the word of a sort of ghost. He's right too, So let's go have a look-see so we have something to tell him."   Steve guided David out to his truck, and then quickly he began to take the roads that David has just told him about. As soon as he was with insight of the old ranger station, he parked his truck just as David said they had already done. Now he notified Gregory McKnight as to where they were going. The two men snuck up as quietly as possible, but all they could see was a man and woman sitting down for dinner. They could not hear what was being said and saw no sign of children. "What if I knock on the door and ask to use the phone because I have a flat tire?"

"That's not bad Steve, one question before you do that; can you see me, or am I invisible?"

"Of course I can see you, you aren't a ghost, after all, so you can be seen,"

"But Deanna was not a ghost and she could be invisible if they can see me

what chance do I have of sneaking up on them?"

"Oh don't worry about that, after all, we only want to use the phone because I have a flat tire."

"Okay, then I will just hang back a little. Wait a minute Steve isn't that the guy that helped you with the kid in the freezer. What is he doing here?"

Steve motioned for Herbie to join them and asked what he was doing here.

"I kept hearing these kids crying and followed the sound, it led to here. What are you doing out here?"

"David was hearing the same thing I guess, so I was following his instinct and try to find out what is going on. I was just about to go up and knock asking to use a phone as I have a flat tire."

"Good idea then David and I can hang back in case something goes wrong."

" Did I happen to mention there may be troopers out here someplace? I called Gregory McKnight and filled him in, so don't shoot until you see the whites of their eyes."

"I don't do no shooting anymore, you guys saved my life so maybe I need to turn my life around. It ain't easy but I'm getting there."

"Well good for you, see what a difference

you can make. David here and I were both cops, and he was my partner, plus we grew up as friends from the time when we started second grade. Okay now here I go, be ready for anything and be careful." Steve continued up the path to the house. There was a porch that went around to the side of the house, but he kept going to the front door and not seeing a doorbell he knocked. No one came to the door so he knocked again harder this time. He heard someone say 'get in there and keep them quiet.'

There was a heavy-sounding footstep coming toward the door. " Yeah what do you want?"

"I was wondering if I could use your phone? I have a flat tire and need to call my AAA dealer."

"I never heard of no gas stations around here, so go away."

"But Sir," began Steve again. Perhaps if you would at least open the door, it won't take long and they come right out to fix your tire."

"My tire?"

"No Sir my tire, I didn't mean your tire."

"Oh alright come in and be quick about it, my old lady has been sick and don't like nobody around. I truthfully think it is an excuse for not keeping her housework done up." He turned and pointed toward the phone.. Just then he heard a child sobbing uncontrollably and a woman yelling for it to shut up or it would get more of the same.

"Sounds as if that kid is in the dog house. What did she do, put the cat in the dishwasher? I remember when my kid did that, boy there was some screaming going on that day."

"Just use the phone and get out of here. The last thing I need is a nosy guy trying to put his two cents into my business."

"Sorry, I just was saying about my own kid, nothing for you to get riled about." Steve went to the phone and dialed a number then began talking about his supposed flat tire. That done he turned to leave but found the doorway blocked by a big bruiser and another one right behind the first one.

"What in blazes is this guy doing here? Don't you recognize him? You should he put Billy Bob away for ten years, and shot Hank just because his kid was acting up. I ain't seen him in a couple of years, I heard he stole some stuff from the cop's evidence room.   What cha doin here pretty boy, want in on our private business, kids homes. The parents can't handle them so we teach them to mend their ways and be good. No, we don't need anymore in our game, besides I don't trust you. There was something funny about the game you were playing you didn't even have to go to jail, just had your hands slapped, lost some pay for a while is that all? Are you back with the men in blue now or what? Let's not take any chances, let's waste him. Come on pretty boy, let's go out behind the house so we don't have so far to drag you in the woods."

As soon as they got outside and began their trip around the house, Herbie stuck a gun in the big guy's ribs and motioned for him to drop his gun. David slipped up behind the other and nicely asked him to also drop his weapon. But rather than drop it he swung around hoping to overtake David by that move. David anticipated just such a move however and ducked down and then he swung around bringing his assailment right where he needed to be for David to swing his gun up and then as it came down it sort of connected with the man's head near his ear and he went down. Night, night whispered David.

They had caught up with McKnight by this

time and he took over, handing these two slobs to a couple of his men. David motioned for Steve to move away from the others. "Steve, I am sorry but I have to get back to the house as fast as possible". He knew that McKnight was a good man and could handle it from here, but it was imperative that he return home immediately.

Steve told McKnight what was going on, and sped back to the house. "I'm sorry Steve, to be making so much trouble for you. "

"Nothing is too much trouble, we have always been as close as brothers so you know it is alright. Whatever is wrong just hang in there buddy we're almost back to the house. As long as no cops stop me for speeding, if they try I won't stop until we get there. They will have to outrun me and I doubt they can, I've recently had this old truck spruced up sort of and it is fast. Never mind worrying about a ticket we are here." Looking toward David he was out cold. Steve blew the horn hoping to alert someone they were home. He didn't need to worry, because both Amanda and Paula were there and so were both doctors.

"Don't get out Steve, there is a problem back where you were and you have to go back. Doctor King is going with you and we will take care of David."

"Are you sure, I can't do anything here?"

"No you are needed back there and fast, Doctor King is right here ready to go with you, Doctor Roberts is seeing to David. I'm coming too said Amanda, so let's get there it might be a matter of life and death."

Steve sped back, "sorry for the fast ride, but when she said to hurry my lead foot heard her," he laughed.

"As long as we get there fast as it calls for then hurry. I have been in fast-moving vehicles before so it doesn't bother me."

"Well it still scares me and I'm already dead. Is it much farther Steve?"

"No we are almost there but I am driving in farther now, we don't need to sneak up on them. I thought there were only two or three guys in here, and McKnight should have handled them alone, but he has one or two men with him."

Suddenly Herbie was in his headlights, so he turned off his engine and got out. "Where is everyone," asked Steve?

"I've got one guy over here and he is in a bad way. Before you ask I did not call the cops because I was afraid one of them would recognize me and not know I'm a good guy now.

"Alright show the doctor where to go and what needs to be done. I'll be along in a couple of minutes, is it a cop that's hurt?"

"Yeah, and it ain't good either."

Steve grabbed his radio and radioed in "Officer down" make it snappy. He then gave them orders of where they were and hung up so he could help the Doctor.

"Steve I have got to get a message to Kerri, the man in there has been shot in the back at least twice, it's Gregory and she will want to know."

"Never mind, I'm here. I might not be quite dead yet so I don't have the powers you do, but some things are stronger than being a ghost. He's the only man that ever said he loved me, the only person who ever said that to me. He can't die, he just can't," she sobbed.

"Come here and hold this light," said Doctor King. "If you are going to just cry, you won't be of any use to me or to this friend of yours. He has a good chance of making it, but we will need to get him into a hospital. Meanwhile, if those are sirens I am hearing then go and direct them here."

Steve was already on the lookout for the ambulance, and quickly showed them where to find Officer McKnight. He was then rushed to the hospital and Doctor King went with them, as well as Kirra. Without asking or saying a word to her, he had her placed in a bed as well. He ordered a complete list of things, such as blood type, blood pressure, heart rate, and any other things he could think of. He oversaw her hooked up with an IV, Saw to it that she was given a sleeping potion that would give them time to do all of the testing and begin to bring her health back to where it should be. He did not want her fighting his every move and trying to just keep her away from Gregory McKnight. As soon as he felt that Gregory was going to be alright and coming along nicely he had them moved into the same room, much against hospital policy, but for the good of the patients he felt.

Chapter 7

Steve saw the ambulance leave, he decided to check out the house. After all, they were here to check on the children that both David and Herbie claimed to be hearing. He went to the door motioning Herbie to stay back and watch. Then he boldly stepped up to the door and Knocked waiting for someone to come and answer the door. A woman of medium build came to the door with a shotgun aimed at Steve's belt.

"Yeah now what do ya want? Just back up I don't know what you boys have been up to, but you ain't cummin in here. I told the last guy that and when he wouldn't listen I shot him. It don't make no never mind to me who you are or what you want either. I can shoot you as easily as I did that cop."

"I just wanted to come in for a minute so I could maybe use your phone,"

"Hey you're the guy what came in here earlier with some story about a flat tire, and my brother said you was a cop once. Well he took you out of here and now you're back. Where is Joey, what was all that shooting going on out here?"

Steve stepped forward and she raised her gun, but instead of reaching for it to pull it from her hands, he grasped the barrel and pushed her backward. She was off balance because she thought he was going to pull. She fell backward and the gun went off in the ceiling.

"Why you son of a----

"Now that isn't nice talk for a lady. Let me see the other end of this gun, I want to see if it feels different to me, pointing away from my middle. Now get up nice and slow like and let's have a look-see in that other room, where you were hiding the last time I was here. Herbie come on in now, I need your help."

"Well hello Gwenda, how have you been sweetheart? So this is where your sickly mother lives, and you would be gone a week or so to help her. You knew I would understand because you loved me so much there was no reason to doubt you. How is mommy dearest? What is with all those kids? You told me we couldn't have children even though you had wanted one so bad and you loved children."

"Oh shut up you shit for brains, I had to tolerate you because Marvin Harrison told me I had to, so he could keep his eyes on you through me. I never wanted no damn kids, they are just put on this earth to make life miserable."

"Well now Herbie, that is another strike against Mr. Harrison. I just heard your friend Harrison got away when they were rounding up the rest of the gang."

"Good," muttered Gwenda, "He should be here any minute then to get me out of here,"

"You just keep thinking that and see what kind of rude awakening you are about to have. Here Herbie, hold this gun on her while I tie her up. We had better put a gag in her mouth or tape it shut or she will yell her fool head off, and warn anyone that may be outside. Oh, that's good masking tape it should keep her quiet for a little while. Now let's go and find those kids."

Steve found about six in the next room, they were tied and gagged as well. He freed these and started for the stairs.

"Oh please don't go upstairs, we know there are more kids up there but that place is bad, some of them die up there," said one boy.

"Then we need to go upstairs and make sure

no more die. How many more are up there," ask Steve?

"Gee Mister, we aren't supposed to know for nothin, so that way we keep out of trouble. Go on upstairs if you want to, Floyd and Cecil should be up there with more kids and guns. Get shot if you want to, you're probably only here to put us in another camp where we can learn the hard way how to do as we're told."

"Don't say that Billy, you don't really think they would believe you do you? If Floyd is up there it's only for one thing and he has Ella May with him and may kill her too."

Most of the kids were crying by this time and didn't know what to say. They were afraid that if they cried, it was a weakness they were told and they would be punished for it.   "Please Mr. Can we go and find our mothers? Where is that other man, he came right in through the window and began untying us then he would carry one kid out and a second one on his back. He got about six of us out before something happened to him and he never came back. Was he a friend of yours or not? Are you really here to help us or just to get us to another bad place like Billy says?"

" I'm here to help you and so is my friend over there. Just stay as calm as you can, and we will help as many as we can, hopefully, all of you."

"Oh, oh" whispered Billy they heard the ruckus down here and one of them is on his way down now."

"Stay back and don't say anything," whispered Steve. He stood off to one side of the stairs and unless someone had his head turned he wouldn't be noticed.

The man that was coming had a gun out and was trying to step softly as he descended the stairs. As he reached the second step up from the bottom, Steve reached around and grabbed the gun. He gave a hard pull and the man lost his footing and came to rest on the stair post.

"Herbie cover him, I'm going up. And Herbie stop shaking, you've got the gun, he's got a headache and the witch is tied in her den." Steve continued up the stairs, taking them two at a time now. He glanced in the first room and saw no one. He continued on down the hall, finally, he found several girls with no clothes on and trying to hide. "Do you have clothes somewhere close, then get dressed as fast as you can. We are leaving as soon as I check this next room and it is raining out now so you will be cold. Find anything that will help you to keep warm, shoes would help too." As he reached the next room he heard a young girl scream, then he heard a slap.

"Stop fighting me, this won't hurt, at all, you'll like it."

"Not as much as you'll like this," said Steve, as he hit the man with the handle of his gun. He had not hit him hard enough to keep him down though, so he hit him again this time with his fist, but still, the man was getting up. "Keep coming big boy, this gun has more than one end to it. Now just back out that door slowly. Now you can turn toward the stairs and start walking slowly, We have a party going on downstairs and we want you to join in the fun, everything alright down here Herbie"?

"Yes sir and I even used your phone to call for back-up a Mr. Zophy answered. Was that what you wanted me to do?"

"You did good Herbie, in fact so good if you want a steady job you can work for me."

"Okay boss sounds good. But I have a

question, how are we fitting all of these kids in your truck"?

"I didn't think of that, well we have them out of this hell hole, next problem is how to get them all in a car."

"You know this is supposed to be 'Steve and his Ghouls,' well don't I have a say in this?"

"Amanda I forgot for a minute you were here. Sorry, so do you have any ideas?"

"Well for starters let's see how many children we have to transport, then that rain out there isn't letting up at all, so we need more clothes and blankets for these children. Herbert, did Chief Zophy say how long it would take him to get here?"

"Not exactly, he said it was out of his area or something like that, I told him it was you I was calling for and that McKnight had been shot. Then I hung up because I was afraid he would be asking my name and they still don't know I've gone straight."

"Steve I have checked the ropes and the three of them are secured. Now I'll go and find Chief Zophy and let him know about the kids. Do you suppose he will listen to a ghost?"

"I have no idea but he's a good man and he knows what I do, so maybe he will. Just be careful, remember that other guy is still out there somewhere. Sweety pie in there is sure he is coming for her, but I think he will look out for himself."

"Oh yeah call Deanna, she has something to tell you and said it was important."

Amanda left immediately and Herbie and Steve tried to think of how to transport the kids out to safety. He called Deanna, who was very glad to hear from him.

"Amanda just left to get Chief Zophy, we have a lot of kids to transport out of here. I don't know where they are from, but there are 10 or 12, they have welts where they have been punished and lack of food, and few beds and even fewer clothes. I can tell you more about it when I get home."

"Steve, David is not doing great right now, aside from the fact he was ill anyway. He now has pneumonia, and great welts on his back, we are having a hard time keeping him down. He says he needs to talk to you, so here he is." Deanna handed the phone to David.

"Steve be careful of the barbed wire, caught a couple of barbs myself, but I got a couple of kids out and I left them hiding until I could get back for them, It was raining and I had all I could do to see. They are in an old shed out behind that house. They are going to need clothes and food, but I collapsed so I knew I had to get back here. I am sorry I left the hard part for you but the doc, says I'll be fine soon."

"You just get back in bed and follow doctors orders as well as Deanna's and Paula's, it is for your own good. Besides you did more for those kids than anyone else, you are the one that told us where they were. Keep fighting Old buddy, I guess the department is having major trouble explaining where you are, as well as discovering many of your files are missing. They feel it is an inside job because no one else knew where you kept your more recent files. Also, it appears that your hard drive is missing from your computer."

"Oh no if the wrong people find that stuff, they can make it rough for the good guys. How much does anyone know?"

"Don't get nervous old buddy, Paula and

Amanda know their stuff, We have everything safe at the house. I have not gone through it until I knew how you were making out. I'll be home shortly. We've got a lot of kids to get processed first. Put Deanna back on the phone for a minute please and get back in bed, try really hard to follow the doctor's orders also more important follow Paula's orders."

He got Deanna back on the phone and ask for her suggestions regarding the children. "How many children are we talking about?"

"I don't know for sure, but I have located about ten or twelve, and then David told me about five or six more. They have been beaten bad, starved, and some of them sexually abused as well. Few clothes and even fewer shoes or blankets. Baths would probably be appreciated."

"Find out from John if we can take them in until we discover where they belong, we'll of course have plenty of food here for them, we have twelve rooms upstairs and three baths, and a couple more rooms down here if we need them. When I hang up from you I will leave for town and get clothes of various sizes, and shoes we will wait on, so they can get some the right sizes. Also, I will have Allison and Dawn make up some soup and sandwiches to start with, and lots of hot chocolate, and milk. To think I thought getting a couple of cooks to help was silly, but as usual, you were right. Should I see about beds? Maybe bunk or single, and a doctor?"

"Whatever you think, you are a whiz, and I love you. I'll be home as soon as possible."

He went back inside to tell Chief Zophy, what Deanna had said, and then they went together to see about the other kids in the shed.

"I probably should not agree as to the disposition of the kids, but with everything else that is going on as well as the fact there are so many of them. It has been so chaotic, I was confused. I must have slipped up." He laughed at himself as he, tried to make excuses . You will have to transport them yourself so I don't really know how many there are. I may try to get some names at least".

It was over an hour later when Steve piled as many kids as he could get into the van, with some of them sitting on the floor. Then he piled the rest into his truck.

"Of course they all are wearing seat belts and there aren't more than three kids in the front seat of your truck, right?”

“John you have so much paperwork to do, especially writing up those bad boys and that innocent school teacher, so you can’t see in my truck and van especially with this rain coming down hard. So I’ll see you later at the house.” The two men shook hands and then left in opposite directions.

It was nearly three days later before John Zophy came by with a woman from social services to check on the kids. Most of them were doing well, and their bruises were healing, but some of them had needed special medications to help with the healing. As long as the children were now clean and eating well social services said they could remain where they were as they didn’t have places for that many anyway.

Herbie came a short time later inquiring about the job Steve had offered. They talked for quite a while with an understanding. He would work part-time but he must keep a low profile no fighting no drugs and no drinking. Try to stay away from the past ‘pals’, he would agree with Steve and check on his records in case he was actually wanted for any reason. Harrison still didn’t know that Herbie was not dead, and they planned on keeping it that way.

Chief John Zophy got to work several days later and went in search for Sgt. Murphy, one of his officers. He had wanted to go over a case with him, as they had both been working on it together. Not finding him in his office he inquired with one of the secretaries that worked there.

"Sorry Chief, but he is still out on that body they found down by the old canal, it was the second one in less than a week."

"If anyone needs me I'll be down there with him then."

"Chief, before you go someone just reported a body found out behind, a lot of old deserted warehouses. Murphy was called so he may be on his way over there."

"Well where ever he is I'll be there too."

"I don't understand it, and quite frankly it is making me nervous. I'm almost afraid to go home nights," she told him.

Chief Zophy left to find Murphy and see how the case was coming along. It was odd, they rarely had a killing around there. Sure there was the occasional fight at a bar, or over a squabble between a man and his wife, but nothing like this has been. Now here they were with three bodies in a little over a week.

He drove to where the police cars were lined up, and the men were out scouring the woods. He was reasonably sure they were following protocol and being careful to not disturb the possibility of ground evidence. He was still shaking his head at the sight of the body and the surrounding terrain.

"Hey Murphy, what are you doing knocking these guys off for job security?"

"Hi John, nothing as simple as that. We have not found one thread of evidence that connects these guys together. They have all been men, and they were all killed with a gunshot to the head. All fully clothes no sign of foul play, one guy was a retired navy man, one was a school teacher at one time, and we haven't found out as yet who this guy was or why he's dead."

"I think I can help you with this one, I recognize him. He played in a band for a while, but that was several years ago and not here, it was about fifty or so miles away."

"I called the coroners office, and Joe, over

there, said to tell you it has to stop he is running out of body bags, and with everybody cutting corners, he is already into his next year's supply."

"Ha ha, there has to be one clown in every town, we have several clowns already so tell him to stop auditioning. I am going to head over to Wilson's place, in case you need me, try not to find more bodies for a while, we wouldn't want to get Joe to get nervous; about no bags."

"Hi there Chief Zophy, no don't answer me, they will look at you funny when they don't see anyone for you to be talking to. Before you ask, yes we know this makes three. So far no one has told us anything, I'll let you know when they do. Keep walking, if you stop so we can talk your men will think you've blown your top. Hey this is fun, I wonder how many people I can bug this way? No you can't act as if you want to talk, the little boys in blue are watching you."

"Stop that, this is a serious case and we don't have any leads so far."

"Were you talking to me chief," ask one of the cops?

"No Stanley, just thinking out loud, it helps clear the head, sometimes. Did you notice that cigarette butt by your right foot? Be careful man a little thing like that might blow this whole thing up and we don't want that."

"Yes Sir, I mean no Sir. I'll try to be more careful."

"Weren't we lucky though, that should have distracted him enough he won't have second thoughts about you talking to yourself. I just threw that butt there I found it over near the body. I doubt it was important it was too fresh. No! I don't smoke, see there are some things ghosts can't do."

"I am going to Steve's in case you want a ride."

"Nah this is too much fun this way. Maybe I will put some ideas into Officer Tom Murphy's head."

"Now Amanda you can't mess ----

"How do you know I'm Amanda? Besides yes I can.   I won't though because I know better than to mess up an investigation. Come on Copper, let's go to Steve's house."

"Stop calling me copper, you know we don't like that much."

"Boy when you're worried about a murder, you're no fun."

"The reason I knew you were Amanda is you talk more than the rest of them do."

"Thanks a lot, I think you're great too."

"I'm sorry, that's not what I meant. I can't believe I'm sitting here in my own car driving down the road and talking to a ghost as if you were real. People will come after me with butterfly nets."

"True but, I'm really here. You can't see me, but you can hear me. I on the other hand can see you quite well and hear you as well. I Did not believe that was possible a year ago. I can watch what goes on and hear many things I wish I didn't have to hear as well. Did you ever see a friend of yours being shot? Or something happening to them, but you were just too far away to help them or for them to hear you? Well, that's what this is like for me. I'd like to greet an old friend but how can I? I still have feelings and would like to love again or be loved. Just the thought of someone putting their arms around me and holding me just for a short time, or to hear someone say 'I love you', but I will never have that because someone decided they were done with me all they wanted in the first place was my money. It was easier to just kill me and then they could have it all."

"Sorry Amanda, I guess I didn't stop and think about all you have been through too. It must be hard for you at times. Well here we are at Steve's place, listen if you ever get feeling down or need to talk you can come visit me and we will both talk."

"Thanks Chief, that is very kind of you."

"Well hello John, what brings you here so early in the morning? Doesn't matter what it is, come on in and have some coffee. Have you gotten any closer to finding what happened to those two men?"

"As a matter of fact it is even worse than we thought there is a third one."

"Same as the other two? What did they have in common?"

"I'm honestly stumped so far, one was a retired naval officer, about five foot six, dark hair, thin build happily married. The next one was a school teacher, but I don't think he has taught for a while. His mother got sick, cancer I believe so he

104

quit teaching to stay and help her until the end. I don't think he ever got back to teaching, he's writing books I guess. We don't have anything on this last guy,

"He used to play drums with this band quite some time ago as I recall.   They don't even look anything alike. This guy was six foot two and blonde the second one was sort of a reddish color quite a lot overweight. So it wasn't their build's or hair color and not their job choice. Of course, they could have been going together as partners or business associates, but we haven't found anything as yet. We haven't found any trace of drugs on any of them so far. We are still tracking all leads.

"Steve you were a good cop, why did you give it all up?"

"I was taken out of it through no choice of my own, and then took classes as a private eye. I actually sort of fell into this job. I like where I am now, less rules to go by. Did you get anything that we discussed, if it is necessary we'll go by your rules?"

"Yeah sort of, he was there but no one will talk, so I suggest we put him on probation for a while. Now I have a serious question for you. You and David Miles were friends even before you both joined the force. You were then partners on the force. All common knowledge, next is as his best friend why haven't you been looking for him? Bugging the station or trying to discover why no one is even talking about his disappearance? In my book it can only mean one thing, you know where or what happened to him,"

"John I would tell you if I knew.   In a way, I suppose I do, but only partly. I will tell you what I know, but it must be off the record and you have got swear you don't say anything. If the wrong people learned or found out at all, a lot of other people could suffer.'

"But if this is police business, I can't keep it a secret, even you know better than that."

"Come with me, need I tell you to be very quiet? This is one of the main reasons why I haven't revealed where he is to anyone before this. John, we need to find what happened to David or at least who ordered this done. Thus far I haven't been able to help him, and I really need him here alive."

"Well then we really need to get started and-

"There's more. I hate to say anything about this to anyone as yet. Come back out to the kitchen and have another cup of coffee where we can talk better. John he is not just asleep. He wakes up and starts to carry on a conversation as if he only stepped out of the room briefly. Then the next time he has no idea where he is or how he got here. He doesn't recognize anyone not even me. But, and this is the strange part, I can be ready to rescue like those kids or the girls, and he is there too, He sort of appears and wants to know why I didn't call him. This last thing with the kids, before I knew for sure about them, he made it around the house until he found a window, then went in and began carrying the kids out two at a time in the rain as well as the fact it was dark.   He went through a fence with the kids to an old shed where he told them to stay quietly until he came back for them, several trips later he came around where I was. Told me he had to go back to the house immediately something was wrong. I told Gregory McKnight I would be back as soon as possible, but I had an emergency to see about first. It wasn't until much later I learned he had large tears in his back from the barbs on the fence also he some how managed to get shot. The bullet wound wasn't serious except for the fact he was still recovering from, old wounds and the barbs on that fence were very old and rusty. He passed out then but made sure I knew where the other kids were hidden.   It was him waking up hearing those kids crying. That's how we found them and managed to save as many as possible. He went with me and directed me where they were, but didn't know he was there at first. But still he managed to get in where the kids were and smuggle some of them out. That woman was there and didn't even know he was doing it. Then he somehow realized he was hurt again and found me to take him home, he even found time to help me with a couple of goons that had the drop on me, Only then did he tell me he had to be back immediately. Sometimes he seems to leave his body sort of like a ghost does, but then the next time he takes his whole body with him. None of us can understand it, nor can the two doctors figure it out. Figure it out? Hell, a year ago I would have locked someone like me up for even talking about ghosts. You are a regular guy, and I'll bet you don't believe in them either,"

"I don't believe in ghost exactly, but none of us can explain some things that happen. I have been here often enough lately that I know something is a little odd here. Also off the record, but I know the one you call Amanda can be very persuasive when she wants to be. I think I can hear her and most of what she says makes sense. Don't tell her I said that, I can't see her or anything like that, but I know she's there."

"Yeah, because I talk more than the rest of them."

"There, see what I mean?"

"Oh no that means you have been accepted into this strange place too."

"I've got to go, after all we have three dead men to start figuring out about. I'll hold off about David Miles for a while, that's about all I can promise. Goodbye Amanda where ever you are."

"Hey Zophy, there are a couple guys that are mad about you having anything to do with saving those kids, not to mention rescuing those girls. Look deeper into all the evidence you have on some of the arrests you have made recently. That's all I can find out but I will float in from time to time as I learn more. Oh yes one more thing, one person that is affiliated with these murders is a cop and another holds public office. So be very careful, we tried to warn David too, but he wouldn't listen."

Chief Zophy returned to his office and began reading all of the files they have gotten thus far.

Several days later a cryptic note floated down onto the Chief's desk, as he was sitting there. He nonchalantly picked it up and quickly scanned it before running it through his shredder. "Do not use your phone, come back to Amanda's house something old something new as soon as possible."

John Zophy nodded his head that he understood, glanced around his office, grabbed a couple of pieces of paper, put on his hat, and left telling his secretary he would probably be gone for the afternoon. He took his own truck instead of a police car. Even if the note hadn't warned him, he had found enough to make him even more cautious. What should have taken about fifteen minutes stretched out closer to a half-hour. Using the upper driveway, he drove to the back of the house and parked out of sight of the road. Amanda had been watching for him and opened the door almost before he got out of his truck.

"I see I was expected," he said aloud to no one. "I sort of thought Steve was the one who sent for me, or at least David.   But I guess I have always been a sucker for a pretty face, unfortunately, I can't see a face pretty or any face otherwise. Hello Amanda, I know it is you by all the things you aren't saying but sure want to. I assume I'm here to see Steve, so just lead me to him."

"I can't, he isn't here, and neither is David. They left here about two this morning. We weren't worried until they didn't come back or even call. Steve has left orders if he should come up missing, I was to give you all of David's files as well as his own. That was only if they were gone over twenty-four hours and not even a phone call. So it has been only twelve hours yet. Should we wait another twelve hours or start going through the papers now. Or just go out looking for him? That's why I contacted you, I figured you know more about legal stuff then I ever could."

"It was you telling me to go back over my own records the other day, wasn't it? I did as you suggested, and found some little things that might be important later on. But first I need a case to build on, and I don't have enough yet. If we went out this minute we wouldn't know which direction to start looking in. So let's begin to look at only Steve's latest files."

I'm not sure about that, he only said David's files."

"If Steve gets mad it can be only at me, so I

can get a court order allowing me to see them if I have to."

" I don't really know which files I should get for you, But we will begin with Steve's files."

John spent over two hours pouring over Steve's notes, he learned a lot and was glad he did. The notes were well laid out and defined, He now knew the answers to a couple of questions that had been plaguing him for some time. However no one would believe some of this in a federal court, they frown on stories with ghosts. After talking with Amanda even James was beginning to believe, after all he was here talking to someone and he did come out here at a   request of an unknown messenger, sight unseen of an unknown source. He decided to read David's files since he was here anyway. Every so often a fresh cup of coffee would appear at his elbow and he would pick it up without thinking.

David's notes were not as neat and organized as Steve's had been. It was his guess that Steve had help, probably his wife or one of the girls. The Girls, even John was beginning to refer to them as the girls, Ghosts, not possible, but then what or who are they? David's notes did list who the head of the organization was or so he surmised, and they must have thought that David was getting too close. So the plan was get rid of David, but make it look like an accident. However, according to David his friend (a ghost, named Paula), was in on everything and managed to rescue him. That last entree was made by someone else. The kidnapping of the girls as well as the children seemed to have nothing to do with his (shall we say accident), medical condition. The notes go back to when Steve met his first ghost and followed up until a couple of months ago. It sure also explains how the cold cases were solved. With the help of Ghosts again.   With these facts in hand John was quite certain that they could get a conviction. However, something must be done about ghosts solving these cases, as well as the fact, in order to prosecute we would need witnesses that could be seen.

Amanda just left John to himself and went to the kitchen to talk to the cook and her helpers. Lucky for Deanna they could afford all of the servants, because

it would have proven to be too much, with friends that would suddenly drop in. It was unknown at least to Amanda what Deanna told the hired help, regarding some of the strange goings-on. There were a couple of rooms that were off-limits, so no cleaning need be done in these. Also when Steve sat at his desk in his study, why did he sit by the hour talking to no one?

David and Steve had left together at about two o'clock in the morning. One of their celestial friends came to Steve explaining as much as they knew. He was also told that David would need to be there as well, and they were sure that David would be fine for this at least. Steve told Deanna he would be gone for a while and not to worry.

"I will have David with me, I left word with Amanda that she was to contact Chief Zophy after an extended absence and to turn all of David's files over to him at that time. Remember I love you, so don't worry until I fly over as you did to me. If I ever do fly, I'm planning on staying here at our house."

"Steve, please don't tease me like that, I will be worried even now. If you aren't back within a reasonable time, I am going in and clean your study from top to bottom. I have already ordered the drapes for that room and the walls will be a pale pink with Darker pink drapes. Maybe even assorted stuffed animals all over everything. In fact, it sounds so nice maybe I will start it today."

Steve laughed at that and grabbing her around the waist he swung her around the room kissing her soundly, he told her he would turn her over his knee if she even touched his room. Steve then hurried down the hall to one of the rooms and knocked lightly. When there was no answer he turned the knob and went in.

"Herbie," he called softly. "Herbie," a little louder. Then he advanced toward the bed, only to find no one there. "Herbie, where in thunder'ation are you? I thought we had an understanding about you taking off until we get a solid bill of health for you?"

As he turned around, he saw Herbie with a towel around his head and dressed in clean clothes. "Good morning Boss, I assume they woke you up too. This is great to be able to take a hot shower and have clean clothes. Oh, were you looking for me? Right here and ready to go, do you have any idea where we are going yet?"

Steve just grinned at him, glad he was still there. "Yeah I'm ready too let's grab some coffee before we leave. I also think that David is supposed to be with us as well."

As they went along the hallway they were joined

by David and they all headed for the dining room expecting only coffee at this early hour. But as usual Deanna did not let them down. Rather than disturb the cook or her helper, Deanna had fixed them all something. There was a large plate of scrambled eggs stack of toast a dish of home fries; as well as bacon and sausage. If I hadn't been in such a hurry this morning there could have been muffins and pancakes as well. There's lots of coffee made too, and I have a thermos bottle of hot coffee for each of you."

Chapter 8

Within a half-hour, they were in the Van heading to the spot that had been relayed to them a short time prior.

"I figure we might as well keep driving this van, I haven't tried to find out who it is registered to. If the wrong people see this thing they may figure it is theirs or someone they know. Of course, I've had it gone over and I think I have added a few new tricks to throw at anyone if it is necessary, By the way how were you two told that you had to wake up and go destination unknown?"

"I don't really know, it was as if you were calling me yelling for me to hurry up and you didn't usually do that much yelling so I figured I was needed fast.   Funny, it felt as if I was climbing back to life as if I were almost dead. But as soon as I felt you needed me, I knew I had to get up and see what the problem was. Also, it is odd that I want to be with Paula 'but' and this is a big BUT, how will this work as close as I have been able to figure out I have been in and out of this condition. Unless you have a better explanation I don't know about, this has been going on for months. I'm here and then I'm not, I'm floating like a ghost, but then I'm bleeding from an old rusty barb wire. Unless there is something else I don't know about, Ghosts don't bleed. Is Paula the reason I'm still out of it because subconsciously I'm wanting to die for real so I can be with her?"

"Listen you guys, I don't understand all of this stuff. But I have to work with you two, so is this real or are you in fact a ghost? If you are a ghost, oh well I was nearly one myself. Now I am practicing to use a better speech pattern. All I have ever heard around me since I was a kid in an orphanage, was cuss words and bad mouth for everyone, especially women. But your partner here has been after me to improve, I even have to go straight, do you know how hard that is for me?"

Both David and Steve broke out in gut-wrenching laughter. "Maybe we need to quiet down soon, as we are getting close to our destination. I wonder if I should have sent word to Chief Zophy, and had him join us. No I guess it will be better this way. Oh by the way David maybe I should have asked you first, but it has gone on so long now, I left word with Amanda to turn your notes over to Zophy if we weren't back within a reasonable time slot."

"Good, I should have told you to go thru them yourself, but then I seem to lose all track of time and don't know where I am, nor how long I've been there. Herbie, I remember you from a couple of years back, I thought then that if they ever caught on to what you were doing it would be curtains for you and from both sides. Steve, I don't know if you know this but Herbie has been working undercover for us for a couple of years now. He doesn't like to be called Herbert because that was his old man's name. He was listed as a runaway from an orphanage also a reform school. He went there all on his own, we thought it would be too dangerous, but it didn't stop him. Then he changed and he became tough killed anything in sight. One night after they had gone in after some sleaze ball a couple of the boys grabbed up a couple of young girls and raped them then they threw their body's in a dumpster to rot he hadn't approved from the start, but he left them where they had been thrown. Several hours passed and he had done his share of drinking, but it still played on his mind about those girls. He went back, one of the girls was not dead, but she had given up and felt all she could do was cry. The worst that anyone could do in Herbie's eyes was to let a woman cry. He helped her out and took her to his old home, where his mother could help her. He never understood why his mother stayed with his father. His father beat her regularly, and cheated on her all the time, he even brought some of his women home forcing her to watch everything. Then Herbie came home one night and saw his mother lying in a pool of blood on the floor and the girl beaten as well. There was no help for either his mother or the girl. His father was there drunk or high it was hard to tell and he was passed out."

"Yes he was passed out, the good-for-nothing piece of shit. When he woke up he started calling for my mother and stumbled over her body kicking her as she lay there. Hollering for her to get up off her lazy ass and get him some supper. I grabbed him by his shirt front and was shaking so bad I couldn't even hit him. I have never wanted to kill someone as much as I wanted to kill him that very minute, but it wouldn't bring my mother back or the girl I had tried to save. So don't think I'm that goody guy that David is trying to convince you I am. The worse part was my father didn't get credit for any of it. He claimed that when he got home that was what he found. He admitted he had been drinking a little because of the shock of seeing his wonderful wife like that and he had no idea who the girl was. Water over the dam, let's find out what we are supposed to be doing here."

"Right, spread out and try to hear as much as possible and not get caught. I have a recorder so we can each put in our pockets. Good luck, we'll meet back here within an hour."

"Steve," whispered David. "I recognize that first man as one of the men that was beating me so bad a couple of months ago. "

"Listen if anyone sees us together or hears us, we can all hang not to mention we will be losing a lot of money. This plan began so we could get rid of Steve Wilson. It worked for us until some guy began bringing in some cold cases. That wasn't bad but it turned out that Steve Wilson, an ex-marine had been given the purple cross, and people were beginning to question us. So we had to prove it had all been a mistake, and offer to bring him back on board. His refusing to come back could have been explained away. But our outside man found out that it was in fact Steve that was solving these cases and giving all the credit to David Miles, along with evidence against all of us. We attempted to get rid of Miles, but he has been spotted or he has a double. All we know for sure is he isn't dead and has gotten the facts and some kind of proof against all of us. Now Senator even you with all of your pull won't walk away from this one. What we have to decide here tonight is what are we going to do about all of this."

"What about switching all of the evidence over on Miles, and Wilson? We suddenly prove that we have discovered they were guilty of everything that they think they have on us. We could lay low for a couple of months while the search is on for them to be found. Meanwhile, we as the hero's figure out who those three dead men are and why they are dead. It sure turned out in our favor, when that first man was found. I have no idea who he was or who killed him. But then all it took was someone to kill a couple more so it would look as if maybe one of our missing men had a vendetta against them."

"It might work, but it may take some doing to get the right man for this job. Why did we wait so long to arrest these two guys? It may take a lot of stories but ours will have to be air-tight. Gentlemen, I have the perfect man for the job. This is Marvin Harrison, and he has been here for us from the start. He would appreciate it if the men that had been arrested a while ago were sort of set free. Good men that he could trust, are men that knew who he was and would not stab him in the back."

"Done, now what is your price?"

"Let me first get this straight, how many are

we talking about, and do you mean just roughed up and taken to another state, or do we need to make them fish bait?

"How well known are these men, Senators and some cops come higher than the average vocals. The job will run you a quarter of a million for the big shots, and only $50,000, each for the other ones."

"That's quite steep, isn't it? I mean maybe a couple thousand each sounds like a lot to me."

"Sure we can do it cheaper, but my way is better and nothing will show about any of your connections in this. You can then go right back to your dirty little lives if you want or you can do like he says," pointing to the first man that had introduced Harrison. "Try to talk your way out of all of this. Try and blame a cop that isn't guilty and he will go undercover until he silently has positively proven not only his own innocence but also manage to nail your hides to the cross. So you big boys choose which you want the job done right or a cheap job. Meanwhile how soon can my boys be released?"

"Can we at least talk it over first and then let you know say maybe by tomorrow?"

"Sure I ain't got nothing better to do, but know this the price goes up every day we wait by $10,000. A day for two days and then it goes up $20,000 a day for the next two days, then a $1,000 an hour after that. That is my final offer gentlemen. Good night and I'll be in touch. Old Frank here will always know where to find me, with your final decision."

"Hey who is this guy, I just caught him sneaking around. I didn't see anyone else out there."

"Holy Shit, that is one of the guys we were talking about. Where are the rest of your posse? Don't think you came alone, that would not be the way you work. Maybe we won't need your friend after all Frank. If we have this one there must be others out there somewhere too. Let's get our guns and flashlights and start looking ourselves."

"If there are more out there they could be cops, or maybe your friend that left just as we caught this one. He could be blackmailing us or at least have enough on each of us to blow the whistle. If we go out looking we just might be running into some sort of a trap ourselves. We have no idea how many are out there or how much anyone heard. I think we should put this one away until we need him. Blackmail can work both ways."

"Hey what are we supposed to do now? I managed to get everything on tape, how well did you do? I thought for a minute I was going to get caught," he whispered.

"Yeah that was a little close for comfort," he whispered back. "Do you think we can follow them on foot without being caught ourselves?"

"I'm not sure but if they all drove here, we won't be able to keep up with them and they could get rough with who they already have. It won't do any good to call for backup, too many big shots involved. I think we just have to follow them on foot and try to keep up. They would try to outrun a van, or force us off the road and shoot first and ask questions later."

"Okay, we had best get at it then or we will never even know which way they went.

Chapter 9

"Amanda, now you have got me worried," said John. "I don't even dare go home, According to these reports there are several of us that may get the ax quite literally. I can even see Gregory McKnight is in for it as well. I'm not sure how they will get rid of so many of us at the same time, without it drawing any suspicion to themselves."

"I'm not sure either, but with Senators and Governors and who knows who else is involved, it could be dangerous, to try and fight them."

"Yes, so what would be the answer to the problem? I never signed on to this job to turn my back on crime no matter who was involved. If those of us run and hide, we would be doing a disservices allowing them keep as they are and putting all of the world be in danger. We would have lost everything to a few Hitler types, telling us what to eat, how to prepare what they feed us and the rest of our lives would be spent bowing to and kissing butts. Where would it end? I have never bowed to anyone and can't see myself doing it now either."

"Changing the subject slightly. What do you know about this 'Herbie' guy?"

"Well for one thing he has been an undercover guy working for us. But not everyone on the force knows it. He tells everyone that asks that he lived in an orphanage for a while. Then he claims he was kicked out of a juvenile home. Actually, we pulled him out, as some really bad boys wanted to get rid of him. Now as far as him being an orphan, he sort of was. His father during one of his drunken bouts, where he beat his wife regularly, came home and began yelling and hitting her. When Herbie came in and bounced a heavy pan over his father's head his father only stayed down for a short time. Then when he came to again, he grabbed ten-year-old Herbie by the shirt front and took him to an orphanage explaining that he found him slapping his wife around. He assumed the boy had escaped from some orphanage, so he was just bringing him back. All the way there Herbert Gray had told Herbie, if he didn't behave and stay there he would kill Herbie's Mother. That's why he hated to be called Herbert, as that was his father's name. To help matters along he also told everyone his name was Green.

Turns out his old man killed her anyway and another girl as well. The judge ruled that it was only circumstantial evidence at best. So he turned Herbert Gray loose. This guy Marvin Henderson thought Herbie would be a perfect strong-arm dummy, but when he learned most of the people that Herbie was ordered to waste did not die but some of them turned state's evidence, so he had old Herbie shot. Thing was the guy doing the shooting was a poor shot, so Herbie lived. Now he is back sort of like an underground spy again, but he no longer checks out the bad guys. Instead he is checking out the supposed good guys."

Deanna came to the room a few minutes later, bringing more coffee and sandwiches. Her face held telltale signs that she had been crying. But she brought only a smile with her. "I just got word some of our guys are okay, but one of them has been captured. The message was in a sort of code, one we use to relay important messages to each other. The problem is I don't know who has been caught. Another thing about this is we don't know what they are going to do with the man they have caught. Do they plan on using him as sort of a shield? Or perhaps as a trade but we don't know who or what they would be trading him for. At which time they could shoot him as soon they got their man or men whatever. Sorry, I just had to let you know as much as I did, I just wish I knew what to do."

"Ladies, I also wish I could help, but I am

going home now and will keep in touch with you both. Deanna, I want both you and Krista to stay here at home and as much out of sight as possible. Amanda, there is no problem with telling you to keep out of sight. Take all of these papers both Steve's and David's and put them where no one will find them. Even if someone goes over my head to get a search order, they cannot force you to help them in any way, as they would first have to know you have them someplace. You may be threatened with all kinds of legal actions, but what I am worried most about is they may use Krista or you as collateral or call it a wedge if need be. I will be working on the case from my own office. There are a few people I am certain I can trust, and I will warn them. If I come back here it will only be an emergency and after dark. Only use your cell phones. Amanda if it is possible to bring me news without being seen, but don't take any chances, What am I saying, how can anyone see you? I'm sitting here making plans with a ghost, maybe I'm really off my rocker. I always said I was a sucker for a pretty face, I can't even see your face, and I don't know for sure that you're real or whatever they would call it."

"Hey Copper, I mean John we'll be fine, you be careful." Amanda then used her plasma to make herself visible, just before John left.

"Oh shit, sorry, I meant you are gorgeous there couldn't be enough money in the world to give you up. He would have to have been the world's biggest idiot in the entire universe. Good night Ladies, Amanda thank you for taking the time to listen."

John Zophy, went home just shaking his head. He saw, he heard, he just couldn't believe, what he heard, say nothing of what he saw. Still, with all of that going on he managed to stay alert when he drove home. He spent the next week watching, working, waiting for some sign or word of some sort about David, Steve as well as Herbie. Funny about David, any other man would have died after going through what he had endured. If it hadn't been for his vest, it managed to deflect the bullets and somewhat the knife wounds. But the beating he took would have killed most other men he came in contact with. Then his mind would stray back to the night he had actually seen Amanda. He kept trying to force his mind away from her, there were no such things as ghosts. Maybe he was just tired or working late trying to wrap his mind around the case at hand. He had to find a way to figure out who had been captured, then how to rescue him. So far he hadn't heard from any of the men, did it mean they had all been caught? Or were they laying in the woods or a ditch somewhere bleeding to death? Possibly even dead already. He hadn't heard from Deanna or Amanda either, were they all right? Maybe he had better go over there tonight and check on them."

"But Deanna, this just sitting here waiting is driving us both crazy. What can they possibly do to me, I don't think there are degrees in the death process, either you are or you aren't. Wait a minute before giving me that story about being dead and doing all the things that natural ghosts do. You were in a form of death but those clever doctors brought you back. That isn't the same as being dead, as Paula and I are. Besides Krista needs you more than she will ever need me. Go teach her to cook, or sew maybe crocheting and knitting. You are so important to her and I am sure there are a lot more kids that would love being taught to read and do numbers. What can they do with an education? In time if they begin now, perhaps they can help the children so they will know what to do if they run into some of these same problems."

"Do you mean the babies being born today or tomorrow can understand all of this? But they don't even know who their parents are yet, in fact, they must be like pebbles on the beach."

"This is true, but as you know when we each of us die, only our bodies remain behind. So it is to these 'soles', they are taught goodness and laughter. Also forgiveness and many more things they will need in life today. GOD isn't just a man as we know man to be. He is the laughter in a baby's first gleeful sound, the babbling of a cold mountain stream, he is the sound of the birds and sometimes the song of a bird. He is the soft sound of raindrops dripping down from leaf to leaf, He is all of these things and more, don't make the same mistake as many before you have done, in thinking that you are there to meet a man. Before you leave here your life is pre-destined, and you must decide if you are honest or if there will be hurt in your life, or pain so intense he takes you back to heaven for a refresher course. God allows you to choose your own destination but some of us choose wrong and then blame the almighty for their bit in life. Steve was pre-destined to be there for Krista, and you were the settling force that Steve needed. Paula and I are just here to help you mortals from time to time."

"I understand I think, but how can I help by just sitting here and doing nothing."

"You are doing something Deanna, you are here where he knows he can find you. You're safe and so is Krista, He knows this so it is one less thing for him to worry about. He will be so happy upon his return when you tell him about the baby you are carrying and you must remember that child can pick up one teardrop or headache so you must remain calm. I would suggest you sing to it, but I have heard you sing so I suggest you just put some music on the radio or listen to your cd..”

“Thanks a lot,” murmured Deanna. Besides the baby doesn’t know how I can sing. What do you mean baby? I’m not even sure myself, it is only wishful thinking,”

“Remember we have shared our lives so to speak, and I know many things. I referred to the child as ‘it’ only until either Steve or the doctor decide to tell you. Now just go and relax as much as you possibly can. Paula and I won’t be long and do not let anyone in. I have already told Jason our doorman, and he has balked somewhat as to wearing the bulletproof vest, but he has agreed for your protection and Krista’s.”

Amanda and Paula left soon after this little talk. “Where should we start,” ask Paula?

“Let’s ask a couple of friends if they have seen anything unusual, and go from there”, suggested Amanda.

After questioning several friends and not finding anyone to help them in any way. They gave up and decided to try and learn something on their own, however after a couple of hours searching to no avail, they decided to pay a visit to John Zophy in his office.

"Hello there John, no don't look around we are invisible of course. Have you heard anything as yet? Wait don't answer that question, people will see you talking. Write the answers down and Paula and I can scan them and erase them faster than you can answer."

"Hello, I was coming by the house later this evening, so you are just beating me to it No I have not heard anything.   I think I am even more worried now when even you don't know anymore. I'll be out anyway either later tonight or tomorrow night. How is Deanna holding up?

"Fine, so far. But Deanna has had to hire a couple more girls to help out with all of those kids. She has about 1 4 yet   Some have been placed in homes and are monitored daily by the doctor and a health care woman due to the physical abuse as well as the beatings.   Alright, I will tell Deanna to expect you. I'll probably see you either tonight or soon." And they were gone almost as soon as he turned around.

He wasn't sure what he was looking for then but when he found it he was sure he would sort of know. Suddenly he caught a faint smell of perfume, so he knew he had a guest," Goodbye" he said in an undertone.